"I keep having t[his] fantasy," Kelly murmured

"We're standing here in the kitchen," she went on, "and I kiss you . . . like this." Leaning forward, she traced her tongue over Matt's lips. From his sudden intake of breath, she knew he found the gesture tormenting. "And then you pick me up and take me to my bedroom. . . ."

His heart pounding, Matt scooped her up, carrying her through the darkened house till he reached her bed. "Then what do I do?"

"Put me down. . . ."

"And then?"

Tilting her head, she bit him gently on the arm. "What do you think?"

In *The Homing Instinct*
Elizabeth Glenn paints a wonderfully
realistic picture of small-town Texas.
That's not surprising, considering she's a
native of the state and has always lived
there. Characters and plot, however, are
the products of her imagination, she
insists.

A former counselor and social worker,
Elizabeth is now writing full time—much
to the delight of her editors, who number
among her greatest fans.

Books by Elizabeth Glenn

HARLEQUIN AMERICAN ROMANCE
14–DARK STAR OF LOVE
36–TASTE OF LOVE

HARLEQUIN SUPERROMANCE
67–WHAT LOVE ENDURES

These books may be available at your local bookseller.

Don't miss any of our special offers. Write to us at the
following address for information on our newest releases.

Harlequin Reader Service
901 Fuhrmann Blvd., P.O. Box 1397, Buffalo, NY 14240
Canadian address: P.O. Box 603,
Fort Erie, Ont. L2A 9Z9

The Homing Instinct

ELIZABETH GLENN

Harlequin Books

TORONTO • NEW YORK • LONDON
AMSTERDAM • PARIS • SYDNEY • HAMBURG
STOCKHOLM • ATHENS • TOKYO • MILAN

With love and thanks to Mn,
who has known me all my life
and remains my friend in spite of it

Published September 1986

ISBN 0-373-25224-2

1

KELLY'S FIRST IMPRESSION was that Weatherford looked the same as always—small, sleepy and quiet. Blessedly quiet. She switched off the engine of her red BMW and rested her throbbing forehead against the steering wheel, grateful for the silence. Only an occasional sedate automobile moved along Main Street, and although school had probably been dismissed several hours ago, the Dairy Bar parking lot had been deserted when she'd pulled into it. On second thought, that wasn't exactly normal.

Straightening, she rubbed her temples as she glanced around. Just as she'd thought—no other cars. But the Open sign hung in plain sight on the glass door of the hamburger place. How odd. She narrowed her emerald-green eyes and ran a hand absently through long, thick hair the color of burnished copper. This *was* Friday, wasn't it? Had small-town teenagers' habits changed so drastically since she had been one? She lifted her arm again to check her wristwatch and winced at the aching weariness in her limbs. There was a nagging pain at the base of her neck, spreading down between her shoulder blades, and her legs felt numb.

Four days on the road will do that to you, she thought, wrinkling her nose as she added, *now that you're thirty.*

At the moment, thirty felt ancient. Doug had warned her not to drive all the way from L.A. to Texas alone, and certainly not with a U-haul trailer hitched to her car. He'd even offered to come along and spell her at the wheel. More than once in the last three hundred miles she'd regretted the independent streak in her nature that had made her refuse his help.

But she thought it was just as well she had declined. If Doug had come, the BMW would no doubt have suffered some mysterious and fatal malady before reaching Nevada that would have necessitated their turning back. Somehow Doug would have sabotaged the trip. He thought Kelly didn't have both oars in the water because she intended to give up a successful television acting career and move back to Weatherford, Texas.

Well, she'd come this far without his help. Never mind that every inch of her five-foot-seven frame hurt. She just needed to get out and stretch, to walk around a few minutes and perk up with a cup of strong black coffee. Then she could make it the rest of the way home. Only six more miles to the farm where she'd spent the first eighteen years of her life.

Kelly opened the door and got out, flexing her shoulders in an attempt to ease the stiffness. She started to reach back into the car for her jacket but changed her mind, deciding that her wool slacks and sweater provided plenty of protection. The biting December wind felt good against her warm cheeks, and the trace of dampness in the air made her wonder if it might snow.

Feeling better already, Kelly pushed open the restaurant door and stepped inside, then stood perfectly still, overwhelmed by nostalgia and the pervasive smell of fried onion rings. It *was* the same! The same gray booths—unoccupied for once—along the walls; the same tables and chairs in the middle of the dining area; even the same yellow and red plastic squeeze bottles of mustard and ketchup, placed squarely in the center of each table. Now if only someone from her high school football team would saunter out of the men's room back there and buy her a Cherry Coke....

She grinned and shook her head at the unlikelihood that any of her former classmates still hung out at the Dairy Bar. A moment later, when she turned and saw the tall blond man across the room, she felt as if her fairy godmother had just pulled off a first-class miracle. Despite his added maturity, she recognized him at once. His long-limbed body had filled out and developed a muscular strength that was impressive even in the conservative white button-down shirt and brown tweed trousers he wore. With a negligent grace that intrigued Kelly, he stood there leaning one hip against the counter, displaying wide shoulders, a trim waist, long powerful legs and, from what she could see, a decidedly sexy tush. A ripple of pleasure shimmied through her as she studied his anatomy. Mmmm, yes...the years had been more than kind to him!

It might have been fully a minute later that Kelly managed to drag her eyes upward and realized to her dismay that he had been watching her stare at his derriere. His expression held a mixture of interest and anticipation, with a generous measure of humor thrown in.

She had never been more grateful for her theatrical experience, which enabled her to lift her chin and meet his gaze directly. Big deal. So he had caught her looking. The way his body had turned out, he must be used to it.

Kelly felt her defiance melting as she looked into the warm, soft darkness of his brown eyes. They were beautiful, laughing eyes that could mesmerize a woman and make her forget to notice the rest of his face. But she already knew it was a fine face, a distinctly appealing face, with strong angles, olive-brown skin and a mouth so sensuous it made her shiver. And then, in startling contrast to his dark eyes and skin, there was his hair. In all her years in Hollywood she'd never seen hair like that. It was thick and curly, and just one glimpse revived in her a fierce impulse to touch it. For as long as she could remember she'd wanted to bury her fingers in the spun-silver locks to find out just what it would feel like. Thus far she'd only imagined.

Kelly took a deep breath and smiled again, her brightest smile this time. "Did I ever tell you," she asked as if she'd only been gone a week, "how it thrilled me the time you made that touchdown in the final six seconds of the Denison game, way back when I was a sophomore?"

For a moment he looked surprised, then quizzical. One fair eyebrow quirked, and the corner of his mouth tugged up into a crooked grin as he countered, "Did I ever thank you for going to the senior prom with me?"

Kelly had a difficult time suppressing a chuckle. "I didn't go to the prom with you."

"And I didn't make that touchdown."

"You didn't? You mean that was Luke John?" She shook her head, green eyes sparkling. This was a longstanding joke between them. "I never could tell you apart from that twin brother of yours."

"Then how can you be sure who I am?"

"Elementary, my dear Watson. Since the whole world knows Luke John Kendall is working on his latest movie somewhere in Canada, you could only be the good doctor Matt." She walked toward him with her own long-legged grace until she could smile into those velvet eyes at close range.

He smiled back at her, with remarkable results. Something in his eyes and in his bright white smile zapped her like a bolt of lightning, sending a shock of hot awareness crackling down her spine. In that instant she knew that Matthew Kendall had changed, even if Weatherford hadn't.

So stunned was she by the discovery, her voice came out hushed. "Hello, Matt."

He straightened to his full height of six foot two and reached for her hand, catching her up into a tight hug. For twenty thrilling seconds she was engulfed in his clean male scent and warm strength as she welded herself to his solid length. Then abruptly he held her away, his hands firm on her shoulders as he gazed down into her eyes. "Hello, Kelly. It's been a long time since you were home."

"Six years." She sounded, and felt, breathless.

The pressure of his hands increased a fraction as a small vertical line appeared between his eyebrows. "I'm sorry I missed your mother's funeral."

"Matt, it's all right! You had just started your internship in Houston. I understood why you couldn't come." She didn't mention that at the time he had still been recuperating from his own heart-shattering loss. "Anyway, you sent the most beautiful flowers."

His eyes darkened as she spoke, and she sensed a tension in him that had nothing to do with her mother. Was he remembering that other funeral? She tried to read his face, hoping that wasn't pain she saw. After a moment, he relaxed his grip and rubbed her shoulders lightly. "Six years, Kelly! You're way overdue for a visit."

How would he react to the news that this wasn't just a visit? Strangely hesitant to tell him, she said instead, "I've missed this place."

"You've been missed."

Although she suspected he was just being kind, his words pleased her. She stared deep into his eyes, trying to figure out what it was about him that suddenly made her feel so light-headed. The touch of his fingers on her upper arms? Surely not. In fact, those hands were all that held her up. If he released her now, she would collapse at his feet. Potent stuff, that Kendall magic. And Luke John didn't have it all by a long shot.

"Ahem!"

Kelly and Matt jumped in unison at the sound of a throat clearing. Matt turned back toward the counter, sliding one arm around Kelly's waist. It was a good thing he did, because by then her legs were feeling extremely rubbery. Another result of Matt's charm, she guessed absently.

When Kelly managed to detach her thoughts from the man at her side, she saw that a middle-aged woman stood behind the cash register. Kelly had been too delighted at finding Matt to notice her earlier, but the woman had clearly noticed Kelly. Her homely, weather-lined face wore a look of eager friendliness.

Matt gave her a broad grin. "Hey, Millie, you remember—"

"Lucia!" Millie interrupted with reverent awe. "Lucia St. Claire! I can't believe it! It's really you!"

Kelly managed a weak smile at the mention of the soap opera character she had played for five years. "Hello, Millie. How are you?"

"Wonderful! Just wonderful, now that you've walked in here. I can't tell you how worried I've been about you. Ever since you fell out of that helicopter over the Pacific last month, everybody's been wondering when you'd turn up."

Out of the corner of her eye, Kelly saw Matt's jaw drop. He must be one of the few people in town not to have heard about Lucia's last big scene. "Well, here I am," she said brightly.

"I can see that." Millie propped her elbows on the counter. "But tell me about the show. How were you rescued? Will you pop back up in time to ruin everyone's Christmas? You may be Weatherford's own, but Lucia, honey, you are one wicked lady!"

Kelly searched for words to break it to her dubious fan that Lucia St. Claire, notorious villainess of *California Dreaming*, would cause the good citizens of Soapland no more grief.

"Did Zantini sail by in his yacht and pluck you out of the ocean?" Millie asked.

"No."

"Well, what then? Was it the Coast Guard? A shrimp boat? No, wait! I'll just bet it was a Russian submarine on a spy mission, and you're going to end up sleeping with half the crew before you con them into delivering you back to San Francisco." She paused expectantly. "Well? Am I close?"

"As a matter of fact, no."

"Hey, come on. You can tell me." Millie lowered her voice. "I won't breathe a word, and neither will Matt. He *never* gossips. Says he's not allowed."

Kelly risked a glance at Matt and found him watching her with an intensity that shook her. If she'd had any secrets, his penetrating vision would have uncovered them before very long, she thought with a certainty that left her feeling utterly vulnerable. She had a sudden strong urge to dash outside where at least she might be able to have a lustful thought without his reading her mind, but she doubted if she could move that far under her own steam.

"There's nothing to tell," she said. "Lucia wasn't rescued."

Millie seemed to be waiting for the punch line. When Kelly didn't elaborate, the other woman frowned. "You weren't rescued?"

Matt was studying her too, his eyes warm with unmistakable concern. Too warm. It was much too warm in here, she decided as the room began to grow fuzzy. It was downright hot, in fact, making her sweater stick to her damp skin and her stomach churn with nausea. Suddenly Matt's arm wasn't enough support, and she swayed and reached for him. The last thing she remembered was falling into the dark comfort of his eyes, being swallowed up by a brown velvet sea.

When she came to, she was lying on the floor with something cushioning her head and shoulders. Matt knelt beside her with his fingers on her wrist, head lowered as he focused on the second hand of his watch. Kelly stared in fascination at the shimmering silver halo of his hair, so close that she could have touched it with very little effort. An instant later she caught sight of the scar on his right temple, a patch of white against his otherwise even tan. Roughly an inch square, the flaw usually escaped notice as it was partly obscured by the thick abundance of Matt's hair. As Kelly looked at it now, she wondered for the first time what had caused it.

Lifting her free hand, she reached out to touch his temple, but at the last second stopped. He had turned his head and was watching her, his expression oddly withdrawn.

She snatched her hand back and wondered if the self-assured Kelly West could really be blushing. Matt, darn his hide, was doing the strangest things to her!

"I fainted," she informed him, her voice hoarse.

The tightness around his mouth relaxed. "I noticed."

Millie's worried face, screwed up into one big wrinkle, appeared over Matt's shoulder. "Do you still want me to run down to your office and get your bag?"

"No, thanks. I don't think I'll need it." He made no move to rise or give up his hold on her hand. "When did you eat last, Kelly?"

"Noon." His eyes probed for the truth. "I had a cup of coffee and some crackers." She turned her head to one side so she wouldn't have to face him. The gesture brought her cheek so close to his hard-muscled thigh that she could feel his heat. She gulped. "I wasn't hungry."

"How's your stomach now?"

"Don't ask."

"The last time Lucia fainted she was pregnant," Millie offered helpfully.

Kelly snapped her head back to glare at Matt. "I'm not pregnant!"

He merely looked at her.

"Lucia tried to force Count Alexander to marry her, and when that didn't work she had an abortion. If you ask me—"

"Millie!" Matt's tone quelled the other woman. "Don't you have some work to do?"

"Not really." She paused. "Oh. You want me to be quiet. Say no more. My lips are sealed."

"Thank you."

"Don't mention it. I'll just be in back, making a phone call, if you need me."

"Fine." Matt waited until Millie had gone behind the counter before he laid a palm across Kelly's forehead. "You aren't by any chance feeling achy, are you?"

"A little," she admitted cautiously.

He stroked back a wave of reddish-gold hair from her temple and let his fingers work their way down to her scalp where they began a soothing, subtle massage. "Just a little, Kelly?" he asked in a voice so sympathetic it brought tears to her eyes. "How do you *really* feel?"

Awash in misery, she shuddered. "Rotten! And I'm *not* pregnant!"

"I know that, honey. I'd say you've got the flu."

Kelly sighed with relief. That explained why her muscles were feeling as if she'd just driven a herd of longhorns on foot from El Paso to Fort Worth.

"Where were you planning to stay tonight?"

She hoped he wouldn't stop rubbing her head like that. It felt better than the complete treatment at Body Beautiful. "At home," she mumbled.

His hand hesitated, then resumed the gently provocative stroking movements. "Alone?"

"Of course."

"Does anyone know you're coming?"

She nodded drowsily, her eyelids drooping shut. "I called Cabe Hardwick last week. He's looked after the farm for me ever since Mom died. He said he'd get the utilities turned back on and have his wife go over and clean the place. It should be all taken care of."

"And who's going to take care of you, Kelly West?"

He murmured the question so quietly that she wondered if she'd dreamed it. When she blinked open her eyes, she found him staring down at her with that same warm intensity she had noticed before. "What?"

"Never mind." He removed his hand from her hair, his manner becoming brisk. "Let's get you comfortable."

He helped her up, gave her a moment to adjust to a vertical position, then all but carried her to a booth. "Millie will bring you some chicken noodle soup. You sit here until I get back."

"I couldn't possibly eat any soup. I need to go on home."

"Drink the broth at least. You need the nourishment. I'll be back for you in fifteen minutes. Got that, Millie?" he called.

The waitress-cum-cook hustled out from the kitchen area, looking like a pint-sized drill sergeant masquerading in a Dairy Bar uniform. "Yessir, Dr. Kendall, sir! Soup coming up!"

"What do you mean, you'll be back for me?" Kelly demanded, but the door had already closed behind Matt. She turned to Millie. "Where's he going? I didn't see his car outside. I mean, I didn't see *any* car."

"His office is just down the street. Sometimes he walks over here for coffee when he finishes seeing patients. Now you stretch out there on the seat and rest," Millie urged her, and Kelly wearily did as she was told. Matt had left behind his brown herringbone sport coat, which had pillowed Kelly's head when she had lain on the floor, and now Millie folded it and stuffed it between the wall and Kelly's back. "How's that?"

An enticing, deliciously masculine scent clung to the wool jacket and planted several erotic suggestions in her mind that were highly impractical in view of her present condition. Kelly shut her eyes and banished the naughty thoughts. "Not too bad, considering."

"Considering what?"

"Considering I think I'm dying."

Millie made clucking noises. "Flu can cause a body to feel that way, all right."

"I really can't eat anything, Millie."

The other woman said "Mmmmm" in an agreeable tone, but five minutes later she was holding a cup of chicken broth to Kelly's lips, encouraging her to drink the steaming liquid.

"I never thought I'd see the day when I'd be feeding Lucia St. Claire with my own hands," Millie commented as Kelly sipped. "I *knew* there had to be some kind of justice in this life."

"What are you talking about?"

"The game."

"What game?"

Millie looked astonished that anyone should not know what game. "The regional semifinals, honey. Our high school football team won district, and they're playing Abilene Cooper tonight. I really hated to miss that game. Lord knows just about everyone else went."

"I thought the town seemed sort of deserted."

"Well, now you know why. The boss has a boy on the team, so of course he had to go, and Ellen Smith's girl is a cheerleader. Wilma Baker and I drew straws to see which one of us had to stay and keep the place open, and guess who lost. The way it turned out, Matt's the only customer I've had all afternoon. Until you." Millie's blue eyes danced with excitement. "Wait until they all get back and find out what they missed! Just wait until they see us on the news!"

Kelly felt a distinct sense of unease. "What news?"

"The six o'clock news tomorrow night. Can't have 'em put it on tonight. We've got to be sure everyone's back in town to see it."

"What—"

But Kelly stopped to stare as a blue television news van careened into the parking lot and slammed to a screeching halt next to her BMW. She sat up straight. "Millie, you didn't call the TV station!"

"Now, Kelly, you don't need to thank me. I know how you celebrities love publicity, and I just wanted to help. I guess your career'll be needing a boost since you lost your job on *California Dreaming*. If it'll make you feel any better, you can even tell people you *wanted* to quit the show. No one around here'll be any wiser."

"But I *did* want to quit! It was my idea!"

Millie winked. "That's it, honey. You could almost convince me."

Kelly groaned and raked her fingers through the bright tousled mass of her hair. "I can't be on television, Millie! I look like Godzilla's sister and feel like his grandmother."

"Shush. You look fine." Just then the door opened, and a gangly young man with red hair and freckles ambled in, balancing a video camera on one shoulder. Millie scowled at him. "Took you long enough, Bo Hanover! I thought sure Matt Kendall was going to beat you back here and make off with your biggest news story of the year."

"Hey, Millie. Nice to see you, too." Bo grinned at both of them, then focused on Kelly. "This is it, huh? 'Soap Star Comes Home to Hide and Recover from

Shattered Career'? So you're the famous Kelly West."
He peered at her. "I thought big-time TV stars wore a lot
of makeup. My name's Bo Hanover."

"My career isn't shattered, and I didn't come home
to hide. It's nice to meet you," Kelly said with all the
dignity she could muster as they shook hands.

"If you're not hiding, how come you don't want me
to shoot you?"

"How did you know Kelly didn't want to be on the
news?" Millie asked.

"I've seen that look. Don't see it too often around
here, though. Weatherford's full of hams. Everybody
loves to see themselves on TV." He shifted the camera
and squinted around the room. "Hmmm...let's see
now. Where can we put you so you won't look quite so
peaked, Kelly? The light's going to wash all the color
out of your face."

For the next five minutes she exhausted herself
enumerating the reasons why she couldn't let Bo interview her. Then Millie displayed a previously unrecog-
nized talent for dramatics, bewailing the fact that nearly
everyone in Parker County was at that very moment
eating a burger and fries in Abilene, getting all set to
watch the championship game, while Millie—alas,
poor Millie!—would be the only one in town with no
priceless memories of the day unless Kelly demonstrated what a heart of gold she still possessed. It was
in Kelly's power to grant Millie this one teensy little favor....

In the end, it seemed easier to give in than to endure
any more melodrama.

AS HE PARKED HIS WHITE BLAZER and got out, Matt saw
the van from the TV station and wondered how the me-

dia had got wind of Kelly West's presence here so soon. Unlike Luke John Kendall, Kelly wouldn't have notified them herself. At least Matt didn't *think* she would have, especially not the way she must be feeling. But through the Dairy Bar window he saw the white glaring light that indicated the camera was rolling. He opened the door quietly and went in.

When he had taken in the situation inside, Matt felt a surge of intense, unreasonable relief. It would seem that the TV appearance hadn't been Kelly's idea after all. She sat stiffly erect with Millie's chair pulled close to hers, Millie's shoulder lending her support. The older woman dominated the scene, beaming straight into the camera as she waxed eloquent on the subject of how good it was to have Kelly West back home again.

Matt supposed Kelly could have spoken before he had arrived, but she now looked as if it was all she could do to keep a smile in place on her generous mouth. He studied the unnaturally bright green eyes, fixed rather dazedly in the general direction of the light, then took one look at her pallor and cursed himself for returning that phone call in his office. His nurse could have handled it, and if not for the delay he would have made it back in time to prevent this ridiculous "interview" from happening.

Angry with himself as much as with the others, Matt stalked over to Bo and waved at Millie to get her attention. She responded by talking all the faster, spinning off into a discourse about Weatherford's justifiable pride in the talented entertainers who hailed from there—Mary Martin and her son Larry Hagman, Luke John Kendall and Kelly West.

Matt stopped gesturing and scowled. "That's enough!" he hissed at Millie, who didn't seem to hear him.

Thoroughly exasperated, he stepped between Bo and the women and lifted Kelly to her feet, heedless of the camera's steady whirring. "The show's over," he snapped.

Kelly's lower lip quivered. "Are you mad at me, Matt?"

"I should be. The only thing saving you is that fever you're running." He pulled her to his side with one arm and kept her there, partly because she looked ready to collapse. As for his other reasons for hugging her . . . he noticed the way his adrenaline had started to flow and certain key muscles below his waist were tightening up. Reminding himself of the Hippocratic Oath, he tried to block the definitely sensual messages sneaking over his nerve pathways. What a time for his libido to act up!

Still holding Kelly against him but no longer letting himself dwell on her slender warmth, he turned toward Bo and Millie and the now-silent camera. "You two aren't sick, so what's your excuse? Don't you have any common sense?" Both looked so shamefaced that he softened his tone. "I'm taking Kelly home now. I'll pick up my car later."

"Yes, Matt," Millie said meekly.

"Sorry, Dr. Kendall," Bo added as Matt grabbed his jacket with his free hand and propelled Kelly outside to her car. After retrieving a bulging grocery bag from his Blazer, he got into Kelly's car, too.

Twisting his head to look over his shoulder, Matt frowned at the tricky job of backing up the BMW with the U-Haul trailer behind it. "You must be planning to stay in town a while," he commented.

She gave him an uncertain little smile, markedly at variance with the devilishly seductive grin for which Lucia St. Claire was renowned. Kelly looked pretty much out of it. Obviously she didn't comprehend his reference to the U-Haul, and he didn't bother explaining. "Put your head back and rest, honey," he suggested, and she obeyed, her eyes closing at once.

Matt succeeded in getting car and trailer safely onto the street, then drove quickly and efficiently through the center of Weatherford, heading toward the outskirts of town. Every so often he glanced over at the sweep of copper waves spread out against the white leather upholstery. Kelly's face was half hidden by a glossy lock of silk, but the part that showed deserved all his attention, and he gave as much as he could spare from the highway.

She couldn't be called beautiful, although he figured some columnist somewhere had probably misused that adjective in an effort to classify whatever it was about Kelly West that attracted so many admirers. Even as a little girl she had never been exactly pretty. Her features were too strong, too different. Broad forehead, sharply angled cheekbones and narrow but firm jaw gave her face character, as did her straight, somewhat patrician nose. Her mouth was wide and prone to smile, and she had the eyes of a witch, Matt thought. Heavily fringed with long dark lashes, they tilted up at the outer corners and more often than not seemed on fire with a magical green light. And her coloring—red-gold hair and warm golden brown skin—was as unusual in its own way as was Matt's.

No, she wasn't beautiful. She was striking, vivid, unique—in a word, fascinating. He wondered why he had never noticed that about her before. She hadn't changed much since the last time he had seen her, whenever that was. During college vacation one year? He couldn't remember. It must have been before he had entered medical school, at any rate.

Maybe I'm the one who has changed.

He laughed softly, mirthlessly, and nodded at the thought. Oh, yes, he had changed. Now at least he was smart enough to recognize when he was attracted to a woman who was all wrong for him. And if his body's reactions that afternoon were anything to judge by, he was definitely attracted to Kelly. But that didn't mean he had to get involved with her.

And how did he think he could avoid it, he wondered. By dumping her at her family farm and leaving her there, alone and sick and miserable because she had lost her job?

Way to go, he congratulated himself sarcastically on his dilemma, turning off the highway onto the dirt road to the West farm. Dr. Matt to the rescue again! He could almost hear Luke's mocking laughter in the small car.

The trailer bumped and rattled along behind, making such a racket that Matt expected Kelly to sit up and investigate, but she didn't even flick an eyelash. She must be exhausted.

He sighed and flexed his tight jaw, knowing what he would have to do.

2

KELLY COULDN'T REMEMBER when she had felt so awful. Probably the last time she'd had the flu, which was literally years ago. She'd had her mother to nurse her through it then, to cuddle her and act sad that Kelly was sick.

These days she hardly ever got sick, but when she did there was no one to be sad. Everyone was too busy with their own problems. The thought made her feel even worse, and a single self-pitying tear squeezed out between her eyelids and slid down her cheek.

Don't do that, Kelly, she admonished herself, wiping the moisture away with one hand and sitting up. Ouch! The movement strained muscles that already ached beyond belief. Looking around, she found that she was alone in her warm car, parked in the rapidly darkening dusk in front of the farmhouse that her paternal grandfather had built nearly sixty years earlier. She saw the familiar white frame dwelling with its blue shutters and brick sidewalk leading through dry brown grass to the porch and the three oak trees towering over the yard, and for a moment she was filled with contentment. This was what she had driven thirteen hundred miles to reach.

When she groped for the door handle, a wave of nausea reminded her of her illness, as well as of her utter isolation. She was here on a farm several miles from town, at a house that hadn't been occupied since her mother had died, and she was very much alone. And feeling like hell, she added miserably. If she had listened to Doug, she wouldn't be in this mess.

But she'd had a little help getting into the mess, now that she thought about it. Vaguely she recalled Matt Kendall interrupting the TV interview at the Dairy Bar and rather forcefully escorting her out to her car. And yes, driving away with her. "I'm taking Kelly home," he had informed the others like a knight on a white steed.

She stared through the car window at the deserted farmyard, which was starting to look spooky in a way it never had when she had lived there. "Thanks a lot, Matthew!" she muttered. "Bring me out here and then vanish. I could wither away and die from this blasted bug and no one would ever know."

She tried telling herself that it had been her own idea to stay alone at the farm, and that after all, this wasn't some haunted house; it was the beloved home of her childhood. But in another minute the effects of her flu, her long trip from L.A. and her unexpected loneliness combined to make her dissolve in tears. Since there was no one around to hear, she indulged in a real crying jag, sobbing with noisy abandon.

Suddenly the door beside her jerked open, and she was silenced by a dual shock of fear and frigid air. She lifted her drenched face, expecting to confront a murderer at the very least, and instead saw Matt Kendall bending down to peer into the car. "Is something wrong, Kelly?"

He looked so calm, so completely in charge, that she wanted to hug him. "I . . . I thought you had gone."

"Gone where?"

"Home. Back to town. I don't know."

"That upset you?" He watched her closely. "I could have sworn you said you planned to stay here alone."

"I did. I mean, I do. It just . . . I don't know. I sort of lost my head there for a minute."

One corner of his mouth twitched. "Well, you certainly didn't lose your voice. I heard you all the way inside the house. It sounded like you were dying."

Furtively wiping at her tears, she changed the subject. "Would you look at that! It's almost dark. You probably need to be getting on home now."

"This is your lucky day. I don't have to rush off."

When she heard the amusement in his husky voice, she got all prepared to fight, but the large brown hand that he placed on her wrist stopped her. It was too comforting. Comforting and strong and at the same time disturbing, she thought, astonished at the electric warmth that seemed to emanate from his touch, filling her with a tingling sensation. Had he learned to do that little trick in medical school, or was it something he'd always known?

"Come on, Kelly," he said. "Let's get you settled in the house. I turned up the wall heaters and built a fire in the living room fireplace. It should be warming up by now." When she didn't move, he added as if to persuade her, "The place looks clean, and the beds seem to have fresh sheets on them, so I guess Adeline Hardwick has done her thing."

Slowly Kelly met his gaze again. "You checked to be sure I had clean sheets?" She had never known a doctor yet who was that solicitous of the sick.

He shrugged. "I had to decide where to put you to bed. Let's go in before you get a chill."

Matt held her hand as she got out of the car. An instant later he must have anticipated that her legs planned to mutiny, because he caught her just as she fell, scooping her up into his arms and cradling her against his hard chest.

It felt so dangerously good to be there that she guessed it must be bad for her. Something compelled her to protest. "Put me down. I can walk."

"When did you learn—yesterday?"

"Honestly, Matt!"

"Honestly, Kelly. So far I've been more impressed with the way you fall." He settled her into his arms more securely and strode up to the porch with her.

"Very funny," she huffed, then shut up, exhausted by her feeble attempt at independence. Mmmm...his coat smelled so nice! She rubbed her nose back and forth against the wool and heard Matt chuckle as he maneuvered to open the front door awkwardly with one of his otherwise occupied hands. "What are you laughing at?" she wondered aloud.

"Not a thing. There's a handkerchief in my left hip pocket if you have a runny nose." He used his shoulder to flip on the light switch just inside the door of the entryway, and she saw that he was grinning at her. "I'd get it for you myself, but my hands are full."

Lord, his smile was potent, especially when it happened to be only inches away. Kelly stared at his mouth, then at the silver-gold sheen of his thick hair, then at his eyes where a thousand sparkles of laughter danced wickedly, and found it impossible to be stern with him. "My nose isn't runny," she denied. "I was smelling your coat. I love the way it smells."

"You were smelling my coat." It hadn't been what he had expected to hear. "Exactly what does my coat smell like?"

She cleared her throat, suddenly wishing she hadn't been quite so forthcoming. This was going to sound really weird.

"Kelly?" Matt prompted her.

"You," she blurted, dropping her eyes. "It smells like you."

Maybe he'd blame it on the fever. Come to think of it, it *must* be the fever bringing out the flake in her. She'd never acted like this before in her life. Her usually predictable body was suddenly experiencing all kinds of alarming stimulation—hot and cold shivers coursing through her, thrilling jolts of energy in parts of her that usually demanded very little attention and flash fires burning beneath her skin wherever Matt touched her.

Matt stood frozen in place, holding Kelly easily, not really wanting to put her down and yet hating the weakness that made him need this close contact. She felt utterly desirable, and unless he had misunderstood, she had said she liked the way he smelled, which had the potential to mean a lot more than just that.

No. Don't start reading things into this, he warned himself. Kelly was an accomplished actress who could convey any message she wanted to convey, truth or fiction, through those bewitching eyes. Furthermore, she probably flirted as naturally as she breathed. It didn't mean anything to her. Now Luke . . . Luke was more her type. He wouldn't dream of taking her seriously, which would suit him just fine, because Luke John Kendall had never been serious about a woman in his life.

And *furthermore*, Matt thought grimly, she was sick! End of discussion!

Kelly felt the increasing tension in the powerful arms that gripped her and realized it had been a mistake for her to make that confession about smelling his coat. He must have concluded that she had a fetish for wool herringbone. First thing tomorrow he'd probably start commitment proceedings against her.

Her eyes grew misty, and she shut them and shook her head. She was not going to cry again. Matt didn't need any more proof of her instability.

Before she could get her chaotic emotions under control, his fierce hold on her relaxed, and he began to move through the house. From the snapping flames and the wood-scented warmth, she knew without opening her eyes when they passed through the living room. He had to walk carefully down the narrow hallway, edging sideways to carry her through a doorway and then lowering her onto the turned-down bed. Not her own bed—she could tell by the feel of it. It was the double bed in her parents' room. When she was a kid, she'd loved to take naps in there. The old-fashioned mahogany bedroom suite and lacy white curtains had made the room seem more beautiful than the furniture display at Joske's in nearby Fort Worth.

Opening her eyes, she gazed around the lamplit room while Matt stood back with his hands in his pockets and watched her. By the time she had assured herself that every yellow rose was still in its rightful place on the wallpaper, her tears had dried and her mouth was curving up into the beginnings of a smile.

"Happy memories?" Matt inquired quietly. Her eyes flew to meet his, and she nodded. "Then you'll be okay in here? I knew it probably wasn't your old room, but it's closer to the bathroom than the one with all the purple ruffles."

"I'll be fine in here, Matt. This is perfect. Thank you for your help."

"Don't mention it." Without another word, he turned and left the room, and Kelly stared after him in surprise. Talk about a sudden exit. When she heard the front door open and close a moment later, her smile faded. He hadn't even said goodbye!

Kelly sighed and shook her head. As interested as she was in the subject, she couldn't devote another kilowatt of mental energy to figuring out the enigmatic Matthew Kendall. At the moment the best she could manage was to fall asleep. Maybe her persistent headache would go away if she slept....

She had the strangest dreams off and on all night long. She kept imagining Matt was there in the room with her, giving her Tylenol and sips of cool water, bathing her forehead when she was burning up and putting an extra blanket over her when her teeth began chattering from the chills. She even dreamed that he undressed her and put her into her baggy cotton pajamas, but that part struck her as so farfetched that she just lay back with a tiny smile, enjoying the improbability of it all. If it really *had* been Matt, she hoped he wouldn't have looked at her quite so dispassionately as he took off her clothes. He had acted like a doctor, which might have been a serious blow to her ego if she hadn't realized she was only dreaming.

Thank goodness she did realize that, however, because there were several things she didn't have the nerve to do while awake.

The next time her imagination produced Matt, leaning over her in the glow of the lamp to urge another drink on her, she lifted one hand and plunged her fingers into his hair, tangling them in the fine-textured curls and tugging lightly.

Gratifyingly cooperative, this dream Matt didn't pull back but stayed right where she wanted him so her fingers could wander freely through the silvery softness. The experience was so sensually pleasing that she forgot how bad she felt and smiled up at him. "Silk," she decided with sleepy authority.

"Kelly?" he whispered, his expression quizzical. "What's this all about?"

"I always suspected your hair would feel like silk. Now I know." Burying her fingers deep in the curly thickness, she traced her thumb along his temple and uncovered the scar. "What happened here?" she asked, exploring the rough surface with the pad of her thumb.

"I fell off a windmill and hit my head on a rock."

"That was a dumb thing to do!"

Deep, soft laughter rumbled in his chest. "Mom said the same thing."

She stroked the scar once more, then let her tired hand drop. "It must have hurt."

"Mm-hmm."

Yawning, she shut her eyes. "Hey, Matthew, don't climb any more windmills, okay?"

"I don't plan to."

She fell asleep again, thinking how much she liked his voice. Sometime later she awoke needing to go to the bathroom and somewhat dizzily climbed out of bed. She barely stumbled three steps when Matt's big form loomed in the doorway and took charge just in time to save her from another collapse.

"Kelly, damn it, this is getting to be a habit with you," he growled as he escorted her the rest of the way, hold-

ing her up by the elbows. "Couldn't you have just holl-
ered for me?"

"I thought you could use the practice rescuing me,"
she told him solemnly. She started to close the bathroom door, then poked her head back and grinned.
"You're getting pretty good at it, don't you think?"

She wondered if she would have to dream him up all
over again, but he obligingly waited around for her.
When she came out of the bathroom a minute later, he
was leaning against the opposite wall. Despite the
dimness of the hallway, she noticed that his white shirt
was unbuttoned and the tail hanging out, as if he'd
hastily pulled it on when he'd heard her get out of bed.
The tawny mat of hair covering his chest lured her eyes
down to the narrow point where the hair disappeared
below the waistband of his trousers.

While she was at it, she figured she might as well
study the shape of his tautly muscled hips one more
time. The odds were that he'd look terrific in shorts, or
better still, in nothing. She saw that he was already
barefoot. Maybe if she concentrated hard, the next time
he showed up to rescue her he'd have shed another gar-
ment or two. So far this dream had been more than accommodating.

She smiled with secret anticipation, and Matt
stepped forward to grasp her arm. "Don't get any bright
ideas, Kelly. I've had about all the practice I can handle
for one night."

"Spoilsport," she grumbled as she let him help her
back to bed and tuck her beneath the covers. Before he
could vanish, she caught his left hand and held it up.
As long as she was dreaming, she might as well go for
broke. She'd wondered about this earlier, when the *real*

Matt had been there. "I see you aren't wearing a wedding band."

His face blended into the shadows as he pulled back fractionally. "No, I'm not."

Oops. That was very definitely tension that she felt in his fingers. And his fingers, by the way, were warm and strong—not at all like imaginary fingers should feel. Was it possible she *wasn't* dreaming? Naw!

Nevertheless, she'd better back off. "I, uh, just sort of wondered why," she stammered, trying to be nonchalant.

He withdrew his hand from hers. "I'm not married anymore, Kelly," he reminded her gently.

"I know, but I just thought . . . that is, I've heard . . ." Tears of regret stung her eyes, and she hoped he couldn't see them. "Oh, drat. I'm sorry I mentioned it, Matt. Don't pay any attention to me. It's this fever making me say such stupid things. I'm really sorry."

"Forget it and go to sleep." Hesitating as if he sensed her heartfelt misery, he reached out and touched the tips of his fingers to her cheeks, stroking away the dampness. "Look, I said it's okay." When she just sniffed, he groaned and bent over her, sliding both hands beneath her back to lift her up into a close embrace. His lips skimmed her forehead before he pressed his cool cheek against it to absorb some of the fire burning there. "Kelly, honey, I know the flu is making you feel awful, but please try not to cry. You'll only end up feeling worse." His voice dropped to a gruff whisper against her ear. "I wish I could help you stop aching so bad."

Dazed by Matt's unexpected tenderness, Kelly shut her eyes. Her heart pounded, sending blood racing through her, but oddly enough the added warmth didn't bother her. If anything, she suddenly felt better.

"You *are* helping," she assured him. "I'm going to hate to wake up in the morning and have you disappear for good. You're the best dream I've ever had, although the way you feel I could almost swear you're real." She nuzzled his throat. "Did you know you look enough like a movie star to be one!" Giggling, she added, "Or at least to be his twin brother. Maybe you should go to Hollywood and make a flick. Wouldn't that be wild?"

"Oh, yeah. Wild." Resolutely he let go of her hot body and settled her back onto the pillows, feathering his thumb over her mouth. "Sweet dreams, Kelly," he said with irony, standing up to go.

The joke's on you, Matthew, he thought as he went back to lie down again on the living room sofa. *It wasn't your hair she was caressing—it was Luke John's.*

Stretching out to stare at the glowing embers of the fire, he wished he could push a button and put himself right to sleep. Why couldn't someone come up with a quick cure for the blazing frustration he was suffering from?

Someone had, he told himself dryly. The cure was called sex. And whether or not Kelly West would have been willing to administer the appropriate medicine to Matt Kendall, there was still the Hippocratic Oath to keep him from taking it.

THE PALE DECEMBER SUN had just begun creeping into the bedroom when Matt carried in a cup of hot tea to Kelly. He put the cup on the dresser and went to stand beside the bed, watching her. Her long hair spilled in disarray all over the pillow, a vivid pool of copper waves. One slender hand was tucked beneath her cheek as she slept curled up in a ball like a little girl, her too-thin body hidden by the covers. Her face still appeared flushed, and he hated to disturb her, but he needed to get on to the hospital to check on his official patients—the ones who had come to him seeking treatment, unlike Kelly, who had simply fainted in his arms.

How did he get himself into a situation like this? Luke always said Matt was far too softhearted for his own good, and this certainly seemed to qualify as a case in point. He had spent half the night ministering to, and the other half trying not to think about, a woman who preferred a safe delusion, someone she could confuse with Luke John.

Suddenly he remembered how Kelly had had a crush on Luke way back when they were kids growing up. When she was in the eighth grade and he and Luke were sophomores, Matt had noticed that Kelly always seemed to hang around Luke. She and Matt were friends—close friends, in fact—but he had known it was Luke she adored. Because Luke had had the lead in all the high school drama productions, Kelly had gone out for theater, too. When he had majored in drama at college, she had chosen to do the same, even going so far as to attend Baylor University, where Luke had a two-year head start on her. Matt didn't know if his brother had ever dated Kelly. Probably. Luke had dated nearly everyone at least once. Now Matt wondered, with a peculiar twinge of inner pain, if Kelly could still be fascinated with Luke after all these years.

Well, even if she was pining away for love of Luke, it couldn't possibly make any difference in Matt's life. He gave the best part of himself to his patients, and that didn't leave a whole lot of room for loneliness. He had no plans to get involved romantically, much less to marry again, but if he did he certainly wouldn't pick someone who had been in love with Luke half her life.

And yet he acknowledged that he didn't want to see Kelly hurt. She was his patient, whether or not she had chosen to be, and he felt as protective of her as he would any other sick person in his care—no more and no less.

Okay, he conceded, maybe his concern for her went a little beyond the norm, but it was still within the bounds of friendship.

Annoyed at himself for letting the disturbing mental dialogue go on so long, he sat down abruptly on the edge of the bed. "Kelly?"

She stirred, stretched and moaned when her thigh bumped his hip. It made him feel like moaning too, but for a different reason altogether, and his annoyance promptly doubled. "Kelly, wake up!"

Cracking one eye, she peeped at him, then closed the eye and yawned. "Go away, Matthew," she ordered him, her voice soft with sleep. "It's morning. I can't be dreaming now."

"You're right. This isn't a dream."

Both her bright green eyes popped open at his blunt statement. "What do you mean, it's not a dream?"

"I mean you're not dreaming. You weren't dreaming last night, either."

The expression of horror flashing across her face didn't raise his spirits.

"That was really you? All night long?"

"I'm afraid so."

"Oh, terrific!" She flopped over onto her back and glared at the ceiling, remembering embarrassing snatches of what she had presumed was delirium, pure and simple. She had actually stuck her hand in his hair and played with it! That would just about cinch her reputation as some kind of weirdo. "I thought you left right after you carried me in here. I distinctly heard you shut the front door behind you."

"I went outside to unload the car and trailer. Everything's stacked in the bedroom next door."

Astonished to think a busy doctor like Matt would expend all that time and energy on such a mundane task, she sneaked a look at him. He was staring at his feet, elbows on his knees, hands dangling between his legs. His clothes were wrinkled, his face looked scratchy with a day-old beard and the incredibly silky silver-blond curls were mussed up. He looked as though he'd had a hell of a night, she thought, and all because of her.

"I suppose I ought to thank you," she said, trying to maintain her scowl.

"Don't bother."

"No, really. You did a very nice thing, bringing in all my stuff and then staying here with me, even though I would have been perfectly okay on my own."

"Your gratitude overwhelms me," he said wryly. "Let me get you the cup of tea I fixed and then I'll leave you . . . on your own."

He started to rise, but Kelly grabbed his forearm and stopped him with a burst of strength she hadn't known was in her. Turning his head, he looked at her so intently that the velvety darkness of his eyes did something serious and permanent to her heart. She swallowed hard.

"Matt, please! This isn't easy. After all this time away, I'm not used to such neighborly concern." Terrified that she might cry, she frowned again fiercely. "Did you really expect me to be glad you caught my show last night? I acted like a fruitcake!"

When he silently dropped his eyes to the hand on his sleeve, she was sure her apology would be summarily rejected. But as he stared down at Kelly's tight fingers, a slow grin took over his face, and when he finally looked up at her, the old familiar warmth had stolen back into his eyes. "A fruitcake?" He shook his head, laughing softly. "Personally I found certain aspects of your performance to be . . . mmm . . . inspired."

Kelly was so relieved by the return of Matt's good humor that it took a moment for his words to sink in, and then she asked herself just what aspects he could have enjoyed enough to bring that look to his face. Definitely not her curiosity about his missing wedding ring. That only left her bold foray into hair fondling, or the part where— "You undressed me!" she gasped.

He nodded, making a visible effort to straighten out his mouth.

"Matthew Kendall, you ought to be ashamed of yourself!"

He patted the hand that clutched his arm. "Don't worry, Kelly. I barely noticed you were a woman."

"Thanks a lot!"

He lifted his eyebrows innocently. "I thought that would reassure you. I *am* a doctor, after all."

"What kind of doctor can't tell the difference between a woman and a man?"

"I didn't say I can't tell the difference. I said . . ." His voice trailed off as he eyed her outthrust lower lip with excessive interest. "Did you want me to notice? Is that what you're pouting about?"

"I'm not pouting. And of course I didn't want you to notice! If you think back, you might recall that even when I was six years old I wouldn't let you undress me to play doctor."

"That's right, you wouldn't." The laughter positively danced in his eyes now. "But Jessie Ballinger would."

Kelly blinked. "Jessie Ballinger? Jessie let you undress her?"

"Yep."

He looked so smug and pleased at the memory that Kelly couldn't stand it. She released his arm. "I had no idea Jessie was that kind of girl."

"Oh, yeah. Jessie was pretty wild for a little kid."

"You dated her in high school, didn't you?"

"I sure did." He stood up and walked over to the dresser, returning with the cup of tea. "Here, Kelly. Better sit up and drink this before it cools off anymore."

While he stood over her, arms crossed on his broad chest, she did as he ordered. Handing him the empty cup a minute later, she sniffed. "Well, how do we compare?"

"How do we compare what?"

"How do Jessie and I compare?"

"Huh! That would be like comparing apples and oranges. You've got red hair and she's a blonde. Your eyes are green and hers—"

"I mean," Kelly interrupted with gritted teeth, "how do our *figures* compare?"

Matt pretended to be shocked. "What kind of question is that? I told you, I hardly noticed—"

"Bull corn!" she snapped, a rosy spot of color on either cheek. "I don't care if you are a doctor, I refuse to believe that you're so accustomed to undressing women that you wouldn't notice a few details about my shape. I mean, I may be on the thin side, but I do have one or two minor attributes."

An intriguing glow lit his eyes, and all of a sudden she felt naked. "I can think of at least two," he agreed huskily, letting his gaze drop slowly from her face to her pajama-covered chest. Beneath the white cotton top, her nipples hardened, and she could barely breathe, so sure was she that he could see the thrusting pink tips. "Okay," he admitted, still staring at her bosom, "I noticed. You definitely earned your title."

"What title?" she croaked, thinking that it might be nice to slip her hand between the buttons of his shirt and feel the warm pounding of his heart . . . to run her fingers through the silky tangle of curls on his chest. . . .

"Soap's Sexiest Meanie. Isn't that what they call you?"

"They used to." She wrenched her thoughts back to the conversation, finding it safer than focusing on Matt's lean muscularity. "I guess I'll have to relinquish the crown since I'm now an ex-meanie."

Matt wished he hadn't mentioned the show, but it was too late. He certainly hadn't intended to remind her that she was out of a job. What kind of featherheaded idiots could those producers be to get rid of an adorable villainess like Lucia? Suddenly serious, he leaned over and brushed back a lock of her hair. "Kelly, I need to go to the hospital for a while. How about letting me carry you to the bathroom once more before I leave?"

"Thanks, but I'm fine." *Just go, Matt,* she thought. It would be impossible to rest knowing he was there— that he wasn't a dream. She didn't have the energy to keep imagining how warmly real he would feel beneath her hands, his supple skin covered with springy golden hairs. . . .

"You sure?"

"Positive." Shutting her eyes, she curled up again to show him she meant business.

"I'll have to take your car—"

"Fine. Take it. I'm not going anywhere."

"Would you like me to—"

"No!" She kept her eyes firmly closed. "I wouldn't like you to *anything* except go!" If he didn't, and soon, she might really touch him again, as if she hadn't made a big enough fool of herself for one lifetime.

He watched her for another minute, his lips compressed with a pain he didn't want to feel. She couldn't make it any clearer how she felt about his being there. Obviously she would prefer Luke John.

Grinding his teeth with frustration, Matt left.

3

AFTER TRYING FOR HALF AN HOUR to evict Matt from her mind, Kelly finally stopped fighting the inevitable and settled down to think about him. She never could have believed the teenage Matthew Kendall would turn out to be such a stunningly attractive man. He had always had the fantastic silver-blond hair and trust-inspiring brown eyes and the compelling aura of warmth that drew her like a moth to a flame, but she'd never been so starkly aware that he was male. All her life she'd known he was a dear friend worth cherishing. Now she discovered he was also very sexy. Not in the flashy way that Luke John Kendall was so famous for, but quietly, deeply, powerfully.

With a feeling of impending doom, she suspected Matt's appeal was the forever kind. She would never outgrow it as she had her infatuation with his brother.

Oh, Luke was terrific. Kelly still considered him a friend, someone who would always be special because he was from home. They talked on the telephone occasionally, and if he was in town Luke turned up at every party she attended. Once in a while he took her out to dinner. Luke wasn't the type to forget people from his past, no matter how big or how busy he became. He was determined to reach the top and stay there, but that was nothing new. Aside from getting better looking all the time, he hadn't really changed much from the ambitious kid who had charmed his way through puberty.

But Matt...ah, Matt! He was something else. His charm wasn't the same as Luke's, but it was every bit as potent. In fact, he had all the qualities that seemed to be missing from the plastic playboys Kelly knew in California. If she ever got him in her blood, she feared she'd never be the same again, which made it doubly dangerous for her to be near him because Matt's heart wasn't up for grabs. From everything Kelly had heard through the years, he'd never stopped loving his beautiful bride, who had died in a car accident only six months after he had married her.

You listen here, Kelly, she lectured herself as she plumped up her pillow and tried to find a comfortable position for her aching body. *You're smart enough to avoid getting hurt. Your heart's never been broken yet.* Bruised a time or two perhaps, but nothing drastic. The men she'd known in Hollywood hadn't had that kind of power over her.

Over a long period of time she had found that she wasn't cut out for the life of a television actress. It had been a glittering childhood dream, and she was one of the lucky few who had achieved a measure of success. Many of her supporters, including Luke John Kendall, had told her she could go all the way if she stayed with it, but she had made it far enough up the ladder to learn a few truths about herself. She didn't have to develop an ulcer to know she hated the pressure, the backstabbing and the insecurity. For her the excitement had long since palled, the razzle-dazzle grown tarnished. Confused and disenchanted, she had wondered what could be wrong with her until one day she had woken up to the fact that she had wanted to go home. Not for a visit, but to stay.

It had taken months and innumerable arguments—with herself, with her agent Hal Koenig, with everyone involved in making *California Dreaming*, and especially with her costar, Doug Barron—but she had finally reached the point where everyone else's pleas had failed to move her. She had to do what was right for *her*, and when her contract had come up for renewal, she had known it was right for her to leave the show.

Of course people had assumed she'd simply wanted more money, and the producers had offered her more. A lot more. So much more that Hal had broken open a case of Maalox when she had still refused to sign the contract. Doug had quoted Thomas Wolfe to her: "You can't go home again, Kelly." When that didn't sway her, he had called her a fool.

She had tried to make everyone understand that money had never been a driving force behind her acting. Way back at the beginning, she had been motivated by a desire to please Luke, and then when she had discovered that she did have real talent, she had acted for the pleasure it had given her. It had always been hard work, and she hadn't minded that. But lately she had found herself clenching her jaws just to get through the rehearsals and taping sessions. The parties she had once thought of as glamorous had begun to strike her as unbearably shallow and boring, while Hal had constantly pushed her to socialize more.

A week before she had left, Doug had asked her to marry him. Even though she had recognized it as Alternative Z, or If All Else Fails, she couldn't help being a little flattered. Doug Barron, after all, was a hero to millions of *California Dreaming* fans, the most popular male lead in daytime drama. Having a wife would have cramped his style a bit. Kelly had tried to appear properly touched by his proposal as she thanked him and declined. Her rejection, she had known, had shocked him. He had probably thought she would jump at the offer, having reached the big three-oh.

Kelly wanted love and marriage, all right, but not the Hollywood version. She wanted commitment, fidelity and babies. She wanted to be married to the same man fifty years from now, and she didn't see how she and Doug would have maintained a relationship for a year, unless it was by living separately. She had no regrets about turning down his proposal.

Who knows, she thought, maybe she would happen upon the perfect man right here in Weatherford. There were bound to be some prime candidates among the town's twelve thousand residents. Perhaps not as prime as Matt, but she wouldn't worry about that right now. After all, she was in no hurry. The only thing she wanted to do right now was to recover from the flu, which she would never do if she didn't get some rest.

After a tottering trip to the bathroom, she crawled back into bed and fell asleep without difficulty.

"KELLY?" A cool hand rested for a moment on her forehead, then her cheek. "Kelly, darling, can you hear me?"

The voice, soft and feminine and familiar, penetrated Kelly's sleep-fogged mind. She wiggled deeper into the covers and wondered how Rita Kendall had managed to invade her dreams. First Matt and now his mother. But Matt hadn't been a dream, she reminded herself. That could mean this wasn't, either.

"Kelly?"

"Rita!" She opened her eyes and threw her arms around the lovely brown-eyed woman. "Oh, Rita, it's so good to see you!"

Rita hugged Kelly back tightly. "I'm glad to see you too, honey." She held Kelly away and looked anxiously down into her face. "Do you still feel like you're going to die?"

"Oh, I think I'll live, thanks to your son the doctor. Who told you I felt that bad?"

"Millie. She's told everyone every single word you uttered at the Dairy Bar last night. I guess you know you made her day, fainting like that."

"I'm glad she enjoyed it. Wait until you see the six o'clock news tonight."

Rita chuckled. "The word's out about that, too. To hear Millie tell it your arrival yesterday was the Lord's own form of poetic justice. Together you two have managed to upstage the football team."

"Speaking of the football team, did we win the game?"

Looking amused at Kelly's possessive question, the older woman nodded her head of stylishly short, silver-streaked blond hair. "Yes, we did. Next week we play in the finals. And happy as that makes everyone, there are those who would have preferred to stay in town and see the naughty Lucia St. Claire in person. That's one reason I'm here now."

"To see Lucia?"

"No, honey. To keep everyone else from pestering you. I think Matt had visions of thousands of screaming fans stampeding the place, even though he served notice that anyone who comes out here before you're well will have to answer to him. He wants you to get as much sleep as you can, so he called me from the hospital and asked me to make sure you don't get disturbed. And what do I do? Wake you up practically the minute I walk in!" She made a rueful face. "He's going to kill me."

Kelly laughed, knowing that Matt wasn't likely to stay mad at Rita for long. He adored his mother. "I got a couple of hours sleep, and I'd much rather talk to you." She patted the bed. "If you're not afraid you'll catch my bug, sit down and tell me how you've been."

During the next hour, Kelly heard about Matt's father Tom and the splendid new Hereford bull he'd just bought for his herd, as well as getting caught up to date on news about Tom and Rita's children. Seventeen-year-old Lisa, a high school senior and cheerleader, kept the Kendalls running a dozen different directions with school activities. If that wasn't enough to keep them young, twenty-nine-year-old Jenny and her pharmacist-husband Bill Lewis had two angelic little hellions who could charm the spots off a leopard, according to their fond grandmother. Kelly also learned that Luke John had sent his parents an advance copy of a new record he'd just cut and had promised to try to come home from Alberta for Christmas, and that *someone* needed to talk Matt into going to Lubbock for the football game next Friday night.

"Is that going to be a problem?"

"I'm afraid so." Rita sighed. "One of his OB patients is almost due, and he's worried about her. She's over forty and is going to have to be delivered by cesarean section. Mary's never been able to carry a baby to full term, so she's pretty anxious about it. Her faith in Matt is almost fanatical, which puts a terrible burden on him, bless his heart. He hasn't left town in a month, just in case she should go into labor early."

Kelly bit her lip. "Gosh, Rita, what if she had needed to reach him last night? I don't have a phone out here yet."

"His service could have beeped him. Speaking of which, he called Owen Spears and arranged to have your telephone connected before noon today. Ordinarily they don't do hookups on Saturday, but Matt has a way of getting things done. He told Owen he'll really need a phone tonight."

Rita's twinkling eyes were as disconcerting as her words. Kelly could only surmise that Matt planned to spend another night, and that Rita heartily approved. Feeling an un-Lucia-like blush creep up her cheeks, Kelly tried to think of how to phrase the questions that popped into her head, but Rita didn't give her a chance.

The woman stood up briskly. "Matt said you could eat a little Jell-O or soup, Kelly, and he stocked the kitchen with both. Which would you like to start with?"

Surprisingly Kelly discovered she was hungry, which was a definite improvement over yesterday. "Jell-O sounds good, but I can go to the table—"

"And get me murdered for sure? Absolutely not! Stay right where you are so I can wait on you. Dr. Matt's orders must be followed to the letter."

Rita brought her a dish of strawberry Jell-O, and a cup of tea for both of them, then dragged up a chair and resumed crocheting a half-finished afghan.

As she ate, Kelly admired the intricate design of blue and white yarn. She knew Matt's mother owned a gift shop where she sold locally made goods with a country motif. "Are you going to display that in your shop?"

"No, this one's for Lisa."

"Luke John's told me all about your shop. Don't you carry hand-knit baby clothes?"

"Mm-hm. Things for big people, too. Crocheted shawls and sweaters, embroidered kitchen towels and samplers, handmade place mats, quilts...you name it. We also carry home-canned foods, including watermelon-rind preserves." Once known as the watermelon capital of the world, Weatherford still produced some of the best melons in the country, Kelly knew.

Fascinated, Kelly watched the other woman's fingers fly, lengthening the design. "I'd like to make something beautiful with my hands."

Rita glanced up. "You want to learn to crochet?"

Laughing, Kelly said, "No, thanks! I tried that once and ended up with a monstrosity that resembled a map of the Los Angeles freeway system. What I'd really like is to make a quilt. You know, one of those big, soft, old-fashioned ones with a million different colors in it?"

"You need to talk to Mama. She'd be delighted to help you get started, I'm sure."

"Does Grandma Bowen make quilts to sell in your store?" Kelly asked.

"She makes quilts, but she gives them away before I can persuade her to let me put them in my shop." Rita sounded lovingly exasperated.

Nearly every child growing up in Weatherford had received Annie Bowen's "grandmother" treatment at one time or another—the milk and cookies served up with a generous helping of interest in whatever that child deemed important at the moment. Kelly couldn't wait to see the old lady and share some of her wild Hollywood experiences with her. "I meant to ask, how's your mother's health?"

"Oh, Mama's fine...." Rita's casual assurance trailed off into silence before she sighed heavily. "Why do I keep doing that?" She looked up at Kelly wryly. "Mama's eighty-six. I try to pretend she's going to live forever. I ignore the fact that she's changing, and most of the time everyone lets me get away with it. No one wants to admit she's getting senile."

Kelly put aside her empty dish and leaned across to take Rita's hand. "I'm sorry. I love that lady as if she were my own grandmother."

"She loves you, too." Rita brightened, squeezing Kelly's fingers. "She's just about your biggest fan, you know. Mama has gotten so much pleasure from watching the soap, and from telling everyone over and over how she used to keep you while your mother went shopping, from the time you were just a toddler—how you and the twins and Jenny played so beautifully together."

Kelly released Rita's hand and dropped back against the pillows, grinning sheepishly. "Oh, yes, Jenny and Luke and, uh, Matt were some of my favorite, um, playmates."

Rita smiled absently. "Mama has framed that picture you sent her—the one of the entire cast of *California Dreaming*—and has it hanging on her living room wall. It's the first thing you see when you walk into her house. Only sometimes...well, sometimes she gets confused about which one is you, and she doesn't always remember that your mother has died. Sometimes she forgets to take her high blood pressure medicine and to lock the door at night. That's why Matt lives with her."

Kelly's eyebrows shot up. "He does? At her house in town?"

"Yes. It got to the point where we knew she shouldn't stay by herself. Not at night, anyway. Tom and I tried to get her to move out to the ranch with us, but she's a stubborn old thing. She doesn't want to be a burden, as she puts it, and Matt won't hear of putting her in a rest home. He feels she's better off in her own home, and of course he's right. But darn it, Kelly, I worry about what it's doing to *his* life! It bothers me to see him sacrificing his privacy like this, but we haven't come up with a better solution."

Kelly was thrown oddly off-balance by the news. "He didn't tell me where he was living."

"Well, Matt doesn't complain, but I know it can't be easy for him. When I try to talk to him about it, he says Grandma won't be here forever and that she should spend her last years at home." Tears gathered in Rita's eyes. "You may not have noticed when you kids were younger, but Matt's a hopeless softy. He'll do almost anything to keep someone else from hurting."

Just then the honk-honk of a horn announced the arrival of the telephone man, and Rita went out to tell him where Kelly wanted the phone installed. After the man left, Rita took away the dirty dishes, then returned and asked if Kelly had any unpacking she wanted done.

"I'll do it tomorrow, Rita. I don't want you working."

"It won't hurt me. I should let you sleep."

"I'm not sleepy. I've been thinking about what you said about Matt's tender heart. I wonder... how does he stand being a doctor? I should think all the pain and suffering he sees would bother him terribly."

Rita sat down with a trace of reluctance, her expression grave. "It takes a lot out of him, all right. Matt has a tremendous supply of inner fortitude. He's a tower of strength for his patients, but when he loses one of them . . ." She shook her head slowly. "Oh, Kelly, what it does to him! The problem is that he can't help caring too much. He tries to be objective and stay uninvolved, and usually he manages to fool everyone else, but he can't fool me. After Pete Carpenter's little boy died of leukemia last year, Matt holed up in the cabin at the hunting lease for three days. He lost weight and looked ghastly when he finally came home. He had just got so attached to that spunky little kid."

The enormous lump in Kelly's throat made it hard to sound nonchalant, but she tried. "So Matt, being Matt, would insist on staying with his grandmother. And that spells disaster for his love life, hmm?"

Rita snorted. "*What* love life?"

"Matt's not involved with anyone, then?"

"Matt's involved with half the town, but he's not in love." Her voice dropped to a whisper. "I'm scared to death he'll never let himself love again the way he loved Meredith."

They were sitting together in hushed thought, Kelly wondering why she should feel so terribly desolate, when they heard a car door slam and the clatter of footsteps on the front porch. Rita glanced at Kelly with such pleading guilt that Kelly nodded and put her finger to her lips. Matt was not to know they had been discussing him.

But instead of Matt, it was Lisa Kendall who tiptoed into the bedroom. Finding Kelly awake and visiting with Rita, the small, very pretty girl gave her mother a hug. She half sat on the windowsill, letting one foot swing nervously, and informed them that Matt would be along after he returned Kelly's rented trailer to the U-Haul dealer.

"When did you see him?" Rita asked.

"He came by Grandma's this morning to shower and change clothes before he went to the hospital." For Kelly's benefit, Lisa explained, "I spent the night with Grandma. When we got home from the game last night, Matt's service gave Mom the message that he felt he should stay out here with you."

She spoke so casually that Kelly wondered if it was a common practice for Matt to spend the night with a woman. From what Rita had said about his love life, she thought not. But everyone seemed thoroughly in favor of the arrangement.

"He asked me to drive his Blazer here and get a ride home with you, Mom. I offered to drive Kelly's car, but he wouldn't let me." The impish grin Lisa flashed at Kelly indicated that her initial shyness was fast wearing off. "I don't think he trusts me."

"Matthew trusts you or he wouldn't have given you the keys to his Blazer," Rita said.

"You've got a point." When Lisa smiled, Kelly was amazed at the resemblance to Matt. Lisa had the same warm brown eyes, and her silky blond hair reached midway down her back. "Mom, you haven't forgotten there's a baby shower for Joanne Bendix this afternoon, have you?"

Rita checked her watch, then got to her feet. "Thanks for the reminder. We'd probably better get moving. Are you sure Matt's on his way?"

"Don't worry about me," Kelly said quickly. "I'll be fine by myself. I feel so much better than I did yesterday."

While Rita went to clean up the kitchen, Lisa stood watching Kelly, who still sat on the side of the bed. "I remember the last time you came home. I was eleven, and you hadn't yet become famous."

It had been when Kelly's mother had died. "I remember, too. I noticed then what beautiful hair you have," Kelly murmured.

"And I decided then that I wanted hair like *yours*. In fact, I wanted to be just like you."

Laughing, Kelly combed her fingers through her tumbled mop of curls. "Seeing me like this ought to change your mind. I could stand a shampoo, and I haven't put on makeup in three days." She climbed back beneath the covers and closed her eyes. "Listen!" she whispered urgently.

"I don't hear anything," Lisa whispered back after a moment, and Kelly's green eyes opened in amusement.

"I know. That's what I was talking about. After all those years in L.A., I'd forgotten how quiet it can get here in the country."

"You need some music to keep you company. My radio is in Mom's car. I'll let you use it so you don't start talking to the walls."

A minute later she was back, setting the big portable radio/cassette player on the floor next to the bed and adjusting the antenna. As she switched it on, the room filled with the heart-tugging strains of a love ballad.

"Hey, listen to *this*," Lisa said. "This is Luke John's latest hit. It's about how a man wastes his life mourning his wife who died soon after their wedding night."

The poignant words soon rendered Kelly near tears over the fate of the grieving widower. When it ended, she sighed gustily. "I hope they don't play that one again!"

Frowning, Lisa asked, "Didn't you like it?"

"Sure I did, but I'll have a relapse if I lie around and bawl all afternoon."

An hour later when she heard the song again, Kelly couldn't help noticing the parallels between the musical tale and the tragic end to Matt Kendall's marriage. She knew that Luke John usually only recorded music he had written. Had he composed that particular song? If so, did he intend it to tell Matt's story? And how did Matt feel about it?

She was still pondering that question when Matt finally returned from town. By then Kelly and the radio had moved out to the living room, and she lay on the sofa, bundled up in a blanket and propped against a mountain of pillows.

As Matt's tall, perfectly proportioned form appeared in the door, clad in jeans and a camel-colored bomber jacket, a dozen separate tingles began to creep over Kelly's alert nerve endings. Despite the fact she was lying down, she felt dizzy for the first time in hours. A single ray of sunshine lanced through the window to mesh with Matt's hair, making her blink at the silver-blond brightness.

He hesitated briefly before he crossed the room to where she lay. Shrugging out of his jacket and tossing it onto a chair, he sat down sideways on the edge of the sofa.

Oh, mercy! she thought when their hips touched, *I shouldn't get this excited about a man who's in mourning. It's downright indecent.* She pulled the blanket around her, hoping that would muffle the drumbeat of her heart. Matt reached for her forehead, then let his hand slide down to curve against her cheek, his thumb tracing the line of her jaw. "You look like you're feeling better, Kelly."

She nodded, lowering her gaze from the electrifying warmth of his dark eyes to the equally disturbing width of his shoulders in the soft blue sweater. An image of the way he would look without the sweater and jeans flashed before her eyes—solid muscle and bone, covered by musky olive skin that would smell like his sport coat . . . a sprinkling of golden hair over certain places, leading down to more hair and other delights. . . .

Whoa, she thought. *Hold it! Put those clothes back on him right this minute!* Matthew was there out of the goodness of his heart. He deserved better than to be mentally stripped and devoured.

Her eyes jumped back to his face and then guiltily slid away. "Do you know that in the past hour I've heard six of Luke John's songs on the radio?" she asked brightly.

He withdrew his hand from her cheek and moved back a bit, still watching her but with a measure of reserve in his eyes that hadn't been there before. "You must be listening to the local station. They go a bit overboard on his records. Would you like me to find one of the Dallas stations?"

He started to reach for the radio dial, but she grabbed his hand. "No, don't! I could listen to him all day." Luke's voice sounded so much like Matt's, she could pretend it was Matt on the radio. Another thought occurred to her, and she turned off the radio. "Do *you* sing?"

"No."

His cool tone surprised her. "I'll bet you could if you wanted."

"Let's just say I don't want."

Abruptly he stood up and paced around the room like a leashed tiger. What kind of masochist was he, he asked himself, to hang around while she compared him to Luke John? As soon as she recovered, he'd stay as far away from her as he could. He halted and scowled at her. "What are you doing out of bed? You need to rest."

"I'm not exactly exerting myself, and besides, a person can only take so much rest. I was thinking of washing my hair—"

"Forget it," he snapped. "Maybe in a couple of days."

"A couple of days! I can't wait that long. Look at me. No, don't look!" She clutched her tousled hair with both hands and gazed at him bleakly. "I look awful."

"Don't sweat it," he muttered. "There's no one around to see how awful you look." Luke John was two thousand miles away, for heaven's sake.

No one but you, she grumbled silently. What was he so ticked off about, anyway? "Did you have trouble returning the trailer I rented?"

He looked at her blankly, then shook his head as he took out his wallet. "No trouble at all. Here's the refund of your deposit." He held out several bills.

"Keep it," she said. "I owe you more than that, I'm sure."

"You don't owe me anything."

Matt dropped the money onto the coffee table and sat down on the end of the couch just beyond her toes. Kelly's green eyes took on a smoky haze as she studied the long, outstretched legs in their snug-fitting jeans. Her gaze traveled appreciatively up the length of his well-shaped torso and settled on his profile. She had a ridiculous urge to run the tip of her finger across his silky lashes, and the idea annoyed her into taunting him. "You just being neighborly?"

He flicked a heated glance at her, then looked away again. "That's right." *Care to make something of it*, his expression challenged.

Although she understood her own confusion, she had no idea what was bothering Matt. More than likely he was tired and worried about something. Maybe she ought to tell him she was well enough to stay by herself tonight. It was the truth, and he could use the sleep. But selfish and unwise as it might be, she wanted him to stay.

"Are you sure there was no problem with the trailer?"

"Yes, Kelly, I'm sure." He shifted a little to face her, causing his hard thigh to press against her foot. "Were you expecting trouble? It wasn't stolen, was it?"

Licking her lips, she unobtrusively pulled her foot back just a bit to break the dangerous contact. There! That seemed to help her respiration. "Uh, no, of course not. It just took you longer than I expected. Lisa said you were coming right out after you turned it in at U-Haul."

"I stopped by Dan and Mary Wilson's place first. I had to check on something."

Suddenly Kelly realized what might be causing his moodiness. "Is Mary okay? Your mother told me you're keeping a close eye on her. She *is* the OB patient Rita was talking about, isn't she?"

"Mary's pregnant," he confirmed, running the long fingers of one hand through his thick hair and then rubbing the back of his neck.

Kelly waited for him to elaborate, and when he didn't she asked again, "Is she doing okay?"

"Not as well as I'd like."

She sat up and let the blanket slip open, drawing up her knees and hugging them. The movement brought her near enough to Matt that she could see the lines of fatigue bracketing his sensuous mouth.

"What's wrong?" she asked quietly. "Are you worried about the baby?"

With a visible effort, he put his head back against the cushion and shut his eyes. "The baby will be fine. They'll both be just fine."

She sensed that he was trying to convince himself, and a wealth of tender compassion flooded through her.

"Matt . . ." She inched closer and touched his shoulder. Feeling the sudden tightening of the powerful muscles beneath his sweater, she squeezed gently. "Matt, you're exhausted. You hardly slept last night, thanks to my, er, vivid dreams."

His eyes popped open, but he stared up at the ceiling rather than at Kelly. "Your dreams had nothing to do with it."

"Okay, then, thanks to my flu." She continued to knead the muscles of his shoulder and arm. "The point is, you were up half the night with me. You need to get some rest."

"I can't rest now."

"Why not?"

"I'm too keyed up. Besides, I'm used to losing sleep over my patients. It's one of the hazards of the profession."

Her fingers grew still. "Is that what I am—your patient?"

"Aren't you?" He was looking at her cautiously out of the corner of his eye.

Slowly she began massaging again, working her way up to his neck and then cupping her hand around the back of it, her fingers lacing into the spun-silver curls on his nape. "I don't feel like your patient," she confessed huskily.

"What do you feel like?"

I feel like a woman, she wanted to say. Her hand caressed his warmth, his velvet texture, and her heart flipped over. *And you, Matthew, very definitely feel like a man.* But he was a man who still loved his wife.

"A friend?" she suggested. "An old, good friend?"

His mouth tightened. Trusty old Matt. Dear friend.

But faithful companions weren't supposed to get such a charge out of being touched by old friends, were they? Why, then, did he seem to be on fire with the flaming magic of her fingers? Why did he have the almost overwhelming desire to snatch her long, lithe body up and cradle her against him so he could feel her entire weight pressing down on him, easing the ache inside him?

She rested her other palm on his chest, over his thundering heart. "We are friends, aren't we?" Why was he looking at her like that? The emotions raging deep in those dark, dark eyes frightened her. "Matt?"

He held himself rigid, fighting the effects of her hands, when what he really wanted was to beg her to go on touching him forever. "Yes!" he rasped. "We're friends."

"Then let me help."

"How?"

4

MATT SOUNDED, AND LOOKED, ANGUISHED. "How can you help?"

"Like this." She twisted around to face the back of the sofa and scooted over until her hip fit snugly against his. Putting both hands on his shoulders, with her forearms braced against his chest, she began to rub with slow, soothing skill... to work the kinks out of muscles and tendons that had been tied up in knots for hours. Her fingers crawled up and over and down his back as far as she could reach, while she leaned ever closer to him. Each time she strained forward, the tips of her breasts grazed his soft sweater, and his breathing became more labored. As for her sensitive nipples, they seemed to contain a hundred thousand nerves, each one sending and receiving a different message of sensual pleasure.

"Kelly..." It was a hoarse whisper that could have been easily mistaken for a groan.

She pushed back a little and tried to focus calmly on his smoldering eyes. "Isn't that better, Matthew?"

He made another funny noise and wrapped his arms around her. His strong hands spread out on her back and pulled her forward until she was molded tightly against him, her face buried in the warm curve of his throat. Feeling his pulse throbbing beneath her moist lips, she kissed the tiny sign of life. "Am I helping you to relax?"

"Relax!" This time there was no misunderstanding his agonized groan. Kelly's "help" was driving him wild. He slid his hands down to her waist and pulled her onto his lap, then gathered her as close as she had been before. Now when she lifted her head, his mouth met hers, and at the exquisitely soft touch of his lips, a joyous melting took place deep inside of Kelly.

She closed her eyes and felt herself grow warm and breathlessly happy. Every fiber in her being felt totally alert and at the same time too blissfully content to move except to wind her arms around his neck and nestle closer.

This first kiss was hesitant, a tentative sampling of the sweetness of her mouth. He seemed to be sipping at her, his silken lips moving very slowly and very gently against hers while one of his hands glided persuasively up and down her spine.

After a moment, he drew back his head to look at her through half-closed eyes. She felt feminine and cuddly in his arms as she blinked open her bewitching green eyes and slanted a lazy smile up at him. Had he really ever thought she wasn't beautiful? Ridiculous! Kelly West was the loveliest enchantress he had ever met. And to think he'd known her all his life! How could he have let all these years go by without realizing the extent of her charm? Why hadn't he fallen in love with her and married her instead of Meredith?

To stop that train of thought, he tightened his arms around Kelly and began kissing her as if his life depended on it. Grasping a handful of copper silk at the back of her head, he pressed her hard against him, seeming to need the unreasonable pressure to convince himself she was real. His other hand rested on the small of her back, holding her where he wanted her. Lying back against the cushions with Kelly warm and tangible on his lap, he felt himself come completely alive again for the first time in years.

Like a man who'd been asleep for a long time, he awoke to a deep hunger, not for food but for something almost as basic. Kelly's faintly floral scent and the feel of her slender form in the cotton pajamas stimulated his appetite. Shivering, he slipped one hand up under her loose white smock and ran it over the smooth skin of her back. Dear heaven, she felt good! He was starved for her, and he feared he could never get enough unless he consumed her entire body with his own.

Moaning at the thought, he wrenched his mouth away from hers and pressed his face into her hair, holding her tighter than ever. It had been a long time since he'd wanted anything as much as he wanted to make love to Kelly, and he knew he couldn't. He was a doctor. Doctors weren't supposed to seduce their patients.

A quiet little voice in his head suggested that it wouldn't really be much of a seduction—that Kelly probably wouldn't be averse to making love with him. Wasn't that what her inviting mouth and her willing hands were telling him—that she wanted him, too?

Because I look like Luke John.

The reminder made him flinch. Drawing a shaky breath, he removed her arms from around his neck and set her aside. He got to his feet in one swift movement and strode across the room to kneel by the fireplace and began to lay wood on the grate.

Stunned, Kelly sat where he had dumped her on the sofa, watching his rigid back. What on earth had happened? One second Matt had been kissing her like a man possessed, and the next he was thrusting her away and jumping up to build a fire. Had she done anything wrong? *Something* must have killed his passion.

Rather bitterly she wished her own desire could die an equally hasty death, but she was literally trembling inside with the enormous hunger he had aroused in her.

Maybe that was it. Maybe he preferred his women to be more of a challenge.

She recalled Rita's statement that Matt would never love again as he had loved his wife. That had to be the problem. Matt didn't want a relationship with Kelly or with *any* woman. At least not *that* kind of a relationship. Her spirits sagged, and she curled up on the couch, pulling the blanket up to her chin and closing her eyes.

Darn it all, she shouldn't be so surprised! Ever since Meredith had died, Kelly had been hearing via the Weatherford grapevine how devastated Matt was by the loss—how he had devoted himself to medicine in order to fill the void in his life.

She heard Matt strike a match, heard the kindling catch fire and the blaze explode into a cheerful symphony of crackles and pops, and she felt sadder than ever.

"Kelly," he said, his voice carefully controlled, "would you like some soup?"

"No, thank you." To her dismay, her voice shook and tears burned behind her eyelids. This darn flu had left her emotions in shambles! "I think I'll just take a nap right here." And without opening her eyes, she buried her face in the pillow.

"Are you feeling bad again?"

She wanted to shout at him, *Don't be so nice to me, Matthew! Act like a jerk so I can be glad that I'm nothing special to you!*

"I'm okay," she said.

At her muffled words he wanted more than ever to take her into his arms and keep her there. Obviously she felt terrible, which he would have noticed if he hadn't got so carried away. What could he have been thinking of, to kiss her with such hungry abandon . . . to stroke her and discover just how soft and lovable she was. . . .

When the heat started in his loins and swept up through his stomach and chest to his face, he sank into the nearest chair and covered his eyes with one shaking hand. He recalled the sensation of holding Kelly in his arms and knew he hadn't been thinking at all. He'd been feeling, enjoying, *living* again. He'd been experiencing the first reluctant stirrings of love to disturb his heartstrings since he had read that note from Meredith seven years ago and had learned she had left him.

Several times since then he'd tried to make himself love that way again, but it hadn't worked. Love couldn't be forced, or maybe the problem was that he had lost the capacity to trust. It wasn't so much women that he didn't trust; he didn't trust himself to make a wise choice about love, and he didn't trust love to last.

No one really understood Matt's decision to go it alone. He was aware that people thought he still worshiped Meredith's memory, and it suited his purposes to let them think that, because it tended to stop well-meaning friends from playing Cupid. No one knew Meredith had fallen in love with someone else—that her fatal car accident had occurred after she left Matt. He had kept that information to himself, instinctively protecting everyone involved. If word had leaked out, Matt's entire family as well as Meredith's would have suffered.

By the time he'd finished med school, he'd reached the conclusion that he was better off never marrying again. He put his heart and soul into his practice, investing so much of himself in his patients that he shouldn't feel so empty. He shouldn't, but he did.

He stared at Kelly's huddled body resentfully. *She* made him conscious of his loneliness. She made him want again, and that wasn't good. If she were anyone but Kelly West, he might even think he had a chance. Heaven knows, he'd seen the predatory looks he got from Weatherford's female population. He'd have to be obtuse not to know he was considered highly eligible.

The fact that he looked just like America's favorite heartthrob wasn't much of a blessing, Matt thought. Luke John Kendall was a tough act to follow. The people of Weatherford might appreciate Matt for himself, but the one lady who could make him care only wanted the real thing. She wouldn't be happy with a substitute for very long.

Well, fine. He hoped Kelly knew exactly what she wanted. If Meredith had been as certain of that before they had got married, a tragedy might have been averted. Anyway, Matt didn't have time to waste lusting after what he could never have. He had to keep his mind on things that really counted.

Fittingly enough, his beeper sounded just then, snapping him out of his mental quagmire. He reached for the phone and dialed his answering service, only to hear the message he'd been dreading. Quickly he returned Dan Wilson's call and listened to the news that Mary's temperature had shot up to 104 degrees and that she had begun vomiting. "I'll see you two at the hospital in fifteen minutes," Matt said calmly, and hung up.

As soon as he got another dial tone, he telephoned the emergency room to relay a set of terse instructions for dealing with his patient until he arrived.

Snatching up his jacket, he turned to find Kelly sitting up on the sofa, watching him apprehensively. "I have to go to work for a while. Do you think you'll be okay?"

She took a deep breath. Now was the time to tell him he needn't bother coming back—that she would do just fine without his medical expertise. But something stopped her from saying the words, and she forced a smile instead. "I'll manage. You go on." He started toward the door, and she called after him softly, "Drive carefully, Matthew."

He halted, hearing the unexpected warmth in her voice. For a moment his dark eyes searched her face swiftly while his heart thudded with hope. So often he had heard the same quiet admonition from Tom to Rita, or Jenny to Bill. "Drive carefully," they said, meaning, "I love you."

A bolt of psychological pain slammed through him, making him conscious of a hidden longing so fierce, so intense, that it appalled him. What would it be like to have Kelly bid him goodbye with those words every time he left home, he wondered, and an instant later ordered himself to stop such self-punishing fantasies.

Kelly's smile disappeared at the flicker of anguish in Matt's eyes. His face had gone pale, his jaw tight. One big hand closed up into a fist at his side.

"Matt?"

Her whisper mobilized him, and he turned away from her, pulling on his jacket. "I'll see you later," he said gruffly, and was gone.

Thinking about it as she swung her legs off the couch and stood up, Kelly decided that her choice of words had been unfortunate. *Drive carefully.* That had certainly caught his attention. Maybe he had said that to Meredith just before she was killed.

Kelly groaned and flopped back down on the sofa. No wonder he'd looked so upset.

The idea that she might have hurt Matt Kendall filled Kelly with regret, and at the same time she rebelled against the guilt. How was she supposed to know what she could safely say to him and what was off-limits? Besides, for him to devote himself to his dead wife's memory all these years was a bit excessive, wasn't it? Matt was a strong, healthy, sexy man. He ought to be living a full life by now. He ought to have a lover.

Maybe he does.

Shocked at the intrusive thought, Kelly jumped to her feet and paced the living room nervously. No. He couldn't!

She pictured his long-limbed, hard-muscled form as he'd looked in the jeans and sweater a few minutes ago, and as he'd looked last night with his white shirt unbuttoned, his dark chest exposed to view. Her vivid imagination embroidered details merely suggested by his perfectly tailored pants, and she changed her mind. Yes, he could very well have a lover.

Kelly hated the possibility. Feeling sick at the thought of Matt kissing someone else as he had kissed her earlier, she pushed the subject from her mind and stormed down the hall. Never mind Matt's orders. She intended to wash her hair.

With unflagging energy, she showered, shaved her legs, shampooed and rinsed her hair, then blew it dry. Digging to the bottom of one of her suitcases, she located a seldom-worn peignoir set of ivory lace and satin. When she put it on and studied herself in the long mirror on the bathroom door, she decided the shade made her seem too pale, although the total effect was a definite improvement over the pajamas Matt had found. She was pleased with the firm, high shape of her breasts thrusting against the delicate material that nipped in at the waist and flowed down in graceful swirls around her long legs. To be perfectly honest, she would have been more comfortable in her old flannel robe, but at least now Matt would be able to tell she had a figure.

But he already knew all about her figure, having undressed her, and more than likely he hadn't given it a second thought.

Kelly frowned a little as she ran one fingertip over the fine arch of an eyebrow. Reaching for her makeup case, she selected an eye shadow wand and stroked the smoky-green stick along the upward slanting line of her eyelid. Exotic, alluring, wickedly enchanting...all were terms that had been used to describe her eyes. She didn't agree. To her they looked like hungry cat's eyes.

Expertly Kelly brushed a dab of color onto each cheekbone, adding some highlight to fill out the hollow areas beneath. Until she had come down with the flu, "hungry" had described her to a T. At Hal's insistence she was constantly on a diet, which meant that she was also constantly on the verge of starvation. The *California Dreaming* producers required her to maintain an almost emaciated appearance. If she gained an ounce, Hal quoted the clause in her contract that threatened all kinds of dire consequences if she strayed from the straight and narrow, and he did mean *narrow*.

She chuckled with relish as she realized she wouldn't have to worry about dieting ever again. Just as soon as she got her appetite back, she would go to town and order the biggest, juiciest steak she could find, with all the trimmings. Unlimited trips to the salad bar and a gallon of Roquefort dressing. Baked potato with sour cream and real butter. A dozen slices of toast and, for dessert, cheesecake smothered with strawberries. Mercy! The meal in itself would be worth giving up her career.

Planning future feasts kept her mind safely off the subject of Matt Kendall for another hour. By the time he returned from town, she was once more cozily ensconced on the sofa, listening to quiet music on Lisa's radio. This time she thought she looked somewhat more presentable. Not that it mattered, she hastened to remind herself. Matt wouldn't notice.

Matt did indeed notice, however. He had prepared himself to be utterly detached from Kelly, not liking the way she scrambled his emotions. But the second he saw her propped in regal splendor against the sofa cushions, wearing her elegant peignoir set, something triggered his irrational anger. She looked just like Lucia St. Claire, right down to her perfectly polished toenails. The simply furnished living room wasn't Lucia's natural habitat, but he guessed it would do in a pinch. The stage was set for whatever the sultry, man-eating villainess had in mind.

"Expecting company?" he asked coolly from the doorway. Perhaps she had invited Bo Hanover to do a retake of the interview.

She raised her arms to stretch in a feline gesture that gave her an almost unbearable appeal and made his breath come faster. "No one but you, Matthew. I just tossed a log on the fire." Her smile innocent, she patted the sofa. "Sit down right here and get warm."

He ignored her invitation, even as he tried to ignore his muscle-tightening response to it. If he sat down near Kelly, he'd end up a lot more than merely warm. His temperature must have just risen six degrees as it was.

"You washed your hair," he accused her, coming a scant inch farther into the room.

Reaching up, she lifted a handful of glossy curls and let them sift through her fingers. "Looks better, don't you think?"

"I told you to wait."

She wrinkled her nose. "I couldn't stand myself anymore." Nodding at the Crockpot that he held under one arm, she asked. "What do you have there?"

"Chicken soup. You trying to get pneumonia?"

"Homemade chicken soup? Terrific! Who's the cook?"

"My grandmother. She has this ridiculous notion that you want to get well." His frown deepened. "Was it so damned important to you to look beautiful?"

"I couldn't look beautiful if I tried," she said with a charming lack of concern. "It was important to me to get clean, though. If you take a deep whiff, Matt, you'll find out I smell pretty good now."

He didn't *dare* take a whiff. "You smelled just fine last night."

She grinned impishly. "Thanks. So did you."

Feeling his bad mood start to slip, he forced another scowl. "Yeah, well, you don't follow instructions very well, do you?"

"Nope, but fear not. I promise I won't have a relapse on you. I'm a hundred percent better than I was last night." Her eyes sparkled at him. "The best part is, I'm hungry again. Bring on Grandma Bowen's soup!"

Matt opened his mouth to argue, then closed it in frustration. Shaking his head, he carried the pot to the kitchen and plugged it in. He took out two mugs and waited while the thick stew reheated, all the time wondering why he'd got so annoyed at Kelly. Was it because she suddenly looked like the television star she had been for five years? Last night he'd found himself irresistibly drawn to a vulnerable Kelly West. The white pajamas had made her seem young and unworldly, untouched by Hollywood, and he had liked her that way, without makeup, her hair a tumbled mess. *This* Kelly looked like she was ready to resume her acting career tomorrow. For all he knew, that was what she planned to do. The thought filled him with an unreasonable fear.

When he carried the soup out to the living room, Kelly had turned off the radio and was sitting primly on the sofa with her feet on the floor. He put the tray on the coffee table and sat down beside her. Handing her one mug, he kept the other for himself while he tried to decide how to broach what might prove to be a delicate topic.

Kelly spooned up a bite of the creamy broth with its chunks of tender chicken and made a long sound of satisfaction. "Mmmmmm, this is delicious! You have a wonderful grandmother, Matthew."

He nodded, staring at the fire in silence.

Eyeing his tense profile, she assumed he must be worried about either his grandmother or his patient. "What is preeclampsia, Matt?" she asked quietly.

He turned his head and looked at her in surprise.

"I overheard you on the telephone telling the ER nurse that that was Mary Wilson's tentative diagnosis. Is it very bad?" She read the reluctance in his brown eyes and added, "Look, Matt, let's pretend you're my, um, brother, and you're telling me about the kind of day you've had."

Despite himself, his lips twitched at the suggestion that he should think of Kelly as his sister. He bent forward to put his cup on the tray, then settled back and relaxed. "Okay, sis," he said dryly. "What would you like to know?"

"Could you tell me in general terms what pre-eclampsia means?"

"It's a complication that sometimes develops during pregnancy, for reasons we don't really know. Preeclampsia is one of the toxemias of pregnancy. In other words, it's a condition in which the blood contains a dangerous level of toxins, or poisons."

Kelly ate her soup thoughtfully. "I've heard of toxemia. Isn't that when the expectant mother has high blood pressure and swollen feet?"

"Those are the most common symptoms. Because of her history, I've been seeing Mary weekly ever since her pregnancy was confirmed, and we caught the signs of toxemia right away—the sudden excessive weight gain and elevated blood pressure. I put her to bed a month ago and cut all the sodium out of her diet, hoping that would control her problems, but it obviously hasn't worked."

"What will be done for her in the hospital?"

"For one thing she'll have a nurse with her twenty-four hours a day to make sure she stays in bed. She may have been hedging on that a little at home." Seeing Kelly's raised eyebrows, he explained, "She's been a rancher's wife too long to sit back and pamper herself, as she puts it, while Dan gets his own meals and cleans the house. They've been hit hard by the drought or Dan would have hired someone to help. Anyway, in the hospital she'll also have her blood pressure and other vital signs monitored much more closely, have urine studies done to measure the protein, which can poison the body system, and she'll have her fluid intake and output carefully recorded. If things get worse, we'll be right on top of it."

"How much worse can they get?"

Matt shifted his shoulders restlessly, and his arm brushed hers. Kelly felt the warm touch with an electric awareness that he didn't seem to notice. "A lot worse, I'm afraid. If treatment doesn't prove effective, she could move into eclampsia, which is characterized by convulsions and a comatose state. If that happens, we'll have to take the baby by emergency cesarean section."

Kelly set her empty mug down beside Matt's still-full one and leaned back so her shoulder nestled against his, setting off a dozen new charges of flaring energy within her. Determinedly she ignored the exquisite torment. "Rita said the baby's almost due. Couldn't you go ahead and take it now?"

Idly he picked up her hand and placed it flat on his thigh, stroking the back of it with the tip of his index finger, sending shivers up her arm and through her heart, all the way down to her toes. "Actually the baby isn't due for four weeks. I could take it now if I had to, but from the latest sonogram we can tell the fetus is still small. I want to wait as long as possible so the baby will have a better chance to make it. The closer to full term the delivery, the better prepared the baby will be for survival outside the womb."

Listening to Matt's low voice, Kelly thought how completely competent he sounded—how deeply concerned for the welfare of both the woman and her baby. "Mary's lucky," Kelly murmured, turning her hand over and twining her fingers through his.

He gave her a skeptical look. "Lucky isn't a word I'd use to describe Mary Wilson. Not when it comes to pregnancy, at any rate."

"She's lucky," Kelly repeated stubbornly. "She has you for a doctor."

The expression in his warm eyes turned quizzical, and then he smiled, his teeth white and straight, his mouth unutterably sensual. "I suspect you're prejudiced," he said, "being my sister and all."

Mesmerized, Kelly stared at his mouth, fighting the urge to touch her lips to his in a quest for the provocative tenderness she'd found there before. The feel of his hard, strong thigh flexing beneath her hand sent her heart into overdrive, and a slow flush climbed her throat to stain her cheeks.

"I don't feel like your sister," she said a bit raggedly.

Matt brought her hand up and drew his slightly parted lips along the back of it, nuzzling her flesh, then gently nipping at her wrist with his teeth. "Why do I get the feeling we've been through this before?" He kissed her pulse point. "All right, Kelly, I give. What do you feel like?"

Her wide eyes gazed for a long time into his, their emerald brightness clouding over with uncertainty. Finally she shook her head and gave a small shrug. "Confused, mostly."

"Join the crowd," he said, and pulled her into his arms with a sigh. "Oh, Kelly, you do confuse me!" He burrowed into the clean silkiness of her hair, then chuckled.

Kelly melted against him, loving the blissful comfort of his powerful embrace, his muscled shoulder beneath her temple. "Want to share the joke?" she asked.

"Oh, it's no joke. I just realized how right you were." His voice dropped to a throaty growl. "I took a whiff, and you smell . . . mmmm . . . *nice.*"

Twisting down, she pushed her nose between his arm and side. "Mmmm . . . you, too."

He gave a shout of surprised laughter and yanked her up onto his lap. "Kelly, you nut, that's my armpit!"

"I know. Even your armpit smells good."

She tried to nose her way in again, but he held her away. "Cut it out. I'm ticklish." He pulled her head up onto his shoulder and slid down a little to hold her in a semireclining position. "Listen, honey, I need to talk to you."

She put her arms around his neck and gave a satisfied wiggle. "I'm all ears."

One fair eyebrow arching, he looked over his slender, squirming, adorable armful. "That's not a very accurate description of your anatomy, but I'll let it pass for now. Could we talk about your career?"

"We could, but at the moment I don't seem to have one."

He hesitated. "I'm referring to your TV career."

When he felt her tense suddenly, he told himself he should have been more tactful in approaching this. An instant later, however, Kelly grabbed his arm and pushed up the sweater sleeve far enough to check the gold wristwatch, then sat bolt upright with a squeal.

"Quick, Matthew! It's almost time for the six o'clock news!" She launched herself off his lap and across the room to turn the switch on the television. "Thank heaven you reminded me." As she waited for sound and picture to develop, she fidgeted. "Oh, dear, what if the TV won't work after all these years?"

He sat watching her, not altogether certain that her interest in this broadcast was healthy for her. "It worked well enough last night for me to watch a late movie," he said. "Give it a minute to warm up."

A little doubtfully, she sat back down beside him, only to flash him a relieved grin when the screen snapped into full-color focus and the local anchorman announced the headline news story.

"After a twelve-year absence from Weatherford, nationally known soap opera star Kelly West has returned to her hometown. In an exclusive interview, she talked with our own Bo Hanover about the move."

As the young cameraman had warned, Kelly's TV image was pale to the point of anemia. Her eyes were wide and unnaturally glittery, and her hair had the tousled look of a rock star. Other than that, she told herself sardonically, she looked just fine. At least she maintained a valiant smile through the whole thing. But to call this an interview with Kelly West was a gross exaggeration, because Kelly didn't say two words. Millie talked from start to finish, giving a detailed history of Lucia St. Claire, and then explaining that Kelly had quit *California Dreaming* because she wanted to move back to Texas, to the simple life she'd known as a child. Occasionally Millie looked to Kelly for confirmation of what she was saying, at which time Kelly would nod in response and go right on smiling dazedly at the camera.

Matt's abrupt entry onstage brought the segment to a close. Kelly watched in fascination as the heart-catchingly handsome doctor pulled the feeble villainess to her feet and tucked her securely and possessively against his side while he scowled at the camera. The picture went blank, and the newscaster reappeared on the screen to announce that at that point Dr. Matthew Kendall had whisked Miss West away from the interview to be treated for some undisclosed malady.

Matt stood up slowly and moved over to switch off the TV. Turning back toward the couch, he met Kelly's eyes reluctantly, dreading her reaction. That kind of television exposure would hardly help her floundering career.

Matt's stricken expression was too much for Kelly. She threw herself sideways and buried her face in the nearest sofa cushion, her shoulders shaking. The pillows muffled the hysterical sounds that she couldn't hold back any longer.

A second later she felt his comforting fingers gripping her shoulders, squeezing gently. But when he pulled her away from the cushions, her spirited giggles burst free and filled the room with clear, exuberant merriment. She rested her head on his arm and laughed until tears filled her eyes.

As it dawned on him that Kelly wasn't really crying, Matt held her in puzzled silence, then eased her back down onto the sofa and sat on the edge beside her. He didn't know quite how to interpret her behavior.

It took a while for her to calm down enough to speak. She wiped her eyes and tried to look sober. "Sorry," she finally managed, struggling to keep her mouth straight. "I've never seen anything like that." Just then she lost the battle and broke into another huge grin. "Did you hear what they called me? 'Sophisticated, gracious and glamorous.' Matt, I looked about as glamorous as a zombie!"

He knew if something like that had happened to his brother, Luke John would be hopping mad. But then the media-wise Luke John would never have allowed himself to be interviewed looking anything but his best. Matt reached out and ran his thumb over Kelly's lower lip. "That doesn't upset you?"

Her eyes glowed, as much from his stimulating touch as from her own amusement. "I don't think there's a woman alive who would actually *want* to be seen on TV looking like that, but it's not as if it will affect my future."

Matt stared at her, trying to figure out her nonchalance. Perhaps she thought Weatherford was too far removed from Hollywood for her to have to worry about anyone important seeing the newsclip, but he feared the ridiculous little film had just the right human interest angle to attract the attention of the major networks. The thought of millions of Americans watching Kelly—*laughing at* Kelly—and laughing at Weatherford while they were at it—made him feel sick.

He laid his palm along her jaw and said something that an hour earlier he never would have believed he would say. "Honey, maybe you ought to call the station and tell them you're ready to give them another interview."

"Why would I do that?"

"For one thing, to show everyone that you've recovered from that mysterious illness you're supposed to be suffering."

She shrugged. "Everyone will find out soon enough. I'll run by and say hello to Millie the first time I go to town. She can spread the word much more efficiently than any TV station."

"Luke says . . ." He paused and cleared his throat, finding this more and more difficult. "Luke says every line of publicity a performer gets has the potential to either make or break him. I don't want this one unfortunate little bit of exposure to ruin your chances, Kelly."

"Ruin my chances for what?"

"For another job in Hollywood."

Kelly wondered at the emotions swimming in his dark eyes. He looked as if the words were being forced from him.

"Matthew," she said quietly, "I have no intention whatsoever of working in Hollywood again. I've come home to stay."

5

KELLY WEST...HOME TO STAY.

A hundred different sensations of joy flooded through Matt at the announcement, but before they could fill up the yawning emptiness of his soul, he rejected them. She wouldn't really stay here—not after traveling in the fast lane for so many years. She had achieved what countless others dreamed about. How could she give it up?

His expression grave, he withdrew his hand from her smooth cheek. "Kelly, something happened that made you think you should come home, and that's fine. Everyone needs to do that once in a while...to visit their past. But don't kid yourself that this is permanent. You'll go back." He tried to smile. "I'll give you a week before you start missing the excitement."

Kelly shook her head. "I won't. The only thing I've missed in a long, long time is this place, Matt. Home. Weatherford. People I grew up with." *People I love.*

Resolutely he turned his back on her and stared at the fire. "You're an actress. You'll have to go where the work is."

"I told you, I'm not going to work in Hollywood again. Before you even suggest it, I won't work in New York, either. If that means I never act again, so be it."

He hunched his shoulders and bent forward, resting his elbows on his knees, his chin on one fist. The firelight played on his incredible hair. To stop herself from touching it, Kelly drew her eyes down from the silver curls, down his strangely vulnerable-looking nape, down the powerful slope of his back to his trim waist. Seeing the way the snug jeans rode low on his hips, Kelly had another strong impulse, this time to slip a hand beneath his sweater and flatten it over the warm, supple muscles of his torso.

She forced her eyes back up and focused on his profile. Lord, he was handsome! He also looked sad for some unfathomable reason. Without taking his eyes from the fire, he sighed. "I don't believe that, Kelly."

"Believe it. I've never been more serious."

"You're an actress," he said again, standing up and pacing the room with long, restless strides. "Luke says there's no way to get the greasepaint out of an actor's blood."

Kelly's frustration mounted. She jumped up from the sofa and blocked his path, bringing him to a halt. "Luke says that, does he? And just what makes Luke John Kendall the last word on everything?"

Matt started to brush her words aside with an impatient gesture, then blinked in surprise. She had a point. For the second time in five minutes, he had just quoted Luke—something he hadn't done in years. What was the matter with him? Running a hand through his hair, he asked hesitantly, "You don't agree with him?"

"No. I think it's entirely possible for people to change, to grow. At least I know *I* have. My goals have changed."

He wanted to believe her. More than anything he wanted to think she meant what she was saying. As he gazed down into her tip-tilted eyes, he felt his fierce need liquify and begin to pulse through his veins with a slow rhythm. His heart lurched from intense yearning compounded with a sudden fear that this was somehow just a big misunderstanding on his part. Kelly wouldn't lie to him; he knew that. But maybe she was too confused to know her own mind.

He reached out and grasped her shoulders, his fingers tighter than he realized. "Kelly, the thing is . . . you feel that way now because you lost your job with the soap. It was a blow. You may be angry, hurt, and God knows you have a right to be." His warm eyes transmitted comfort, sympathy, a subtle reminder of her worth as a person. "You were good, honey. You were the best damn villainess I've ever seen. The producers of *California Dreaming* made a big mistake letting you go. As soon as the rest of the industry realizes you're available, your phone will ring off the wall with job offers."

He wasn't kidding; Kelly could see the sincerity in his face and hear it in his soft-spoken voice. His belief in her made her feel very proud. But he had it all wrong. "Matt, you don't understand. It was my choice to leave the show. I let my contract lapse. I told them I'm through."

Frowning, he didn't release her. "You quit? What does your agent have to say about that?"

"Oh, he's not exactly speaking to me these days," she admitted with a rueful grin. "The producers aren't any too pleased with me, either."

"You really quit?"

She watched the cautious hope steal into his dark eyes and felt the desperate heat singe her skin where he gripped her with taut fingers. The way he was acting, she could only suppose her answer was very important to him. Well, of course. With his tender heart, Matt wouldn't want to think Kelly had been fired. He never wanted *anyone* to hurt, much less an old dear friend.

"Yes, Matthew," she assured him. "I quit. I came home because I wanted to. This is where I want to be more than anything—"

Before she could finish, he swept her into an exuberant hug and silenced her with a kiss that took her breath away. His mouth locked onto hers in a merciless assault that momentarily stunned her senses and robbed her of coherent thought. When her bones turned to honey from the unexpected pleasure, Matt's strong arms supported Kelly, held her molded tight to him, her slender satin-wrapped form crushed against the hard masculine planes of his body. His soap-clean scent enveloped her and sent her heart into a joyous spin.

His mouth moved lazily over hers, his velvet tongue stroking and enticing. One arm remained firm around her while the other hand cupped her gently rounded derriere, slid up her tingling spine, then wove its fingers into the shining copper tresses that fell past her shoulders.

He groaned low in his throat, his mouth still fused with hers. Jiggling his hips against her, he let her feel his growing arousal as the kiss lengthened and gathered force.

The knowledge that Matt wanted her planted a tiny seed of purpose within Kelly and made her smile triumphantly to herself. His heart couldn't be shut up in cold storage—not if he reacted like *this* to her nearness. And he couldn't very well deny that he was reacting. His body was all but shouting his response.

Matt's breathing had become harsh, his heartbeat an audible pounding against her chest. He tried to pull his hand out of her hair, only to find his fingers tangled in the silky strands. With a couple of urgent tugs, he managed to free his hand and laid it along her jaw. Warm and strong, his fingers held her face still as he lifted his head to look at her with burning dark eyes.

"Kelly," he murmured, then closed his eyes and shook his head and kissed her again. This time he only brushed her lips with his and then drew his mouth slowly down, tilting her face up with his thumb and tracing the tip of his tongue down her throat to her collarbone. He kissed her there lingeringly, then nuzzled the hollow of her throat as he brought his hand down to caress her breast through the satin peignoir. The clinging fabric hid nothing of her enticing shape, and the nipple hardened in anticipation of his skilled touch. Compliantly his thumb teased the small tight bud with several lambent passes over the crest, setting off tiny explosions of ecstasy in various parts of her body.

Sucking in her breath, she wound her arms around his waist and squeezed. "Oh, Matt!" She buried her nose in his good-smelling shoulder. "Should we be doing this?"

Matt had been a friend to her all her life. At times he had seemed almost like a brother. She didn't want to do anything to risk damaging her relationship with him. But this was so . . . so tormentingly delicious!

"I don't know," he whispered, his breath ruffling her hair. His heart knocked against hers, and his arousal had gone beyond question. "Probably not—" he swallowed "—but I don't want to stop."

"Mmmm . . . me, neither." At the moment he wasn't acting like a man in love with a ghost. He was acting like a man, period. "If this is your way of saying 'welcome home,' I like it very much."

"I like *you* very much," he said, although he was starting to suspect his feelings for Kelly amounted to more than mere liking.

"I want to hear more about that, but can we move this discussion someplace where we'll be a little more comfortable?" She gave him a deceptively innocent smile. "I'm kind of tired. I guess it's the aftereffects of the flu."

His thoughts suddenly racing, Matt escorted her to the sofa and sat her down. He watched her stretch out gracefully on the long cushion. When she reached for his hand, he lay down beside her and wrapped her loosely in his arms, but he remained remote and silent, berating himself. How could he have forgotten so quickly that Kelly had been sick? He had nothing but scorn for doctors who took advantage of their patients' weaknesses, or gratitude, or whatever prompted the physical responses he had sensed from Kelly earlier.

Of course there was always the possibility that she was genuinely attracted to him. *Dear God, let this be real*, he prayed. But he didn't intend to take any chances. He wasn't going to push Kelly for anything until she was completely recovered, and then he would just have to wait and see. If she could separate him from Luke John, maybe these wild, sweet feelings would last. If she couldn't, he'd be better off not getting any more involved with her than he already was. Which was dangerously involved, he admitted with a shiver.

Kelly heard Matt expel his breath in a short sigh that sounded rather impatient. Why didn't he kiss her again?

When he tightened his arms around her and shifted them both so she lay partially on top of him, her pulse accelerated. *Now*, she thought. Now he would take up where they had left off before they had lain down. Instead, he settled her more comfortably along his muscled length and rested one hand on the small of her back. He made no move to explore her with those long, sensitive fingers, nor to instill in her the exquisite awareness that a single feathered touch of his lips could evoke.

Puzzled, she stole a look at his face and saw that his eyes were closed, his straight lashes dusting his cheekbones. Beneath her, his chest rose and fell softly, evenly, and she guessed he had already fallen asleep. He must have been totally exhausted, and with good reason.

Watching him quietly, Kelly forgot her desire in her solicitude for Matt. She sent up a fervent prayer that his beeper would remain silent so he could get a good night's sleep. Maybe she should wake him up and suggest that he move into the bedroom. But he seemed so relaxed, and she couldn't bear to rouse him. Snuggling down against him, she whispered a good-night that was so husky, so tenderly intimate, it took every last shred of Matt's inner fortitude to keep himself from showing her just how wide awake he really was.

KELLY AWOKE ON SUNDAY MORNING in her parents' bedroom, without the slightest notion of when or how she had made the switch. From the looks of the bed, she hadn't shared it with anyone. She couldn't decide whether to feel relieved or disappointed about that. Her mood philosophical, she finally acknowledged that it didn't really matter one way or the other. She had evidently slept so soundly that it would have taken more than a sexy blond bed partner to get her attention.

Speaking of which, where was he? It had been rather pleasant to wake up yesterday to his cup of tea and his concern for her health—once she had got over the shock of realizing he wasn't a dream, that is. As for last night . . . mmmm! It had been even nicer to go to sleep in his arms.

Watching the doorway hopefully, she thought how easy it would be to grow spoiled if Matt looked after her much longer. But of course she wasn't sick anymore. This morning she felt disgustingly healthy, in fact, and she was completely caught up on her rest.

Her travel alarm clock, which she'd retrieved from a suitcase and had placed on the chest of drawers, informed her that it was ten o'clock. There was no way Matt could still be sleeping. Throwing off the covers and stretching, she got out of bed and went to see if there was a doctor in the house.

There wasn't, and her reaction to that discovery was acute disappointment.

She did, however, find a note from Matt propped against the telephone, saying he would call her later. There was also a week's supply of groceries in the kitchen, three casseroles in the refrigerator and a warm quiche on the stove—courtesy of Rita, unless Kelly was mistaken.

Kelly ate a huge slice of the delicious ham-and-cheese dish, then called Matt's mother to thank her. The phone rang ten times before Kelly decided the family must be attending church services. As she ran a tub of water and dumped in a handful of gardenia-scented bath salts, she toyed with the idea of driving the two miles to the Kendall ranch that afternoon to express her gratitude in person.

At one time she wouldn't have hesitated to do so. As a teenager, she had often spent the night with Jenny Kendall, who was a close friend despite being a year younger than Kelly. Back then Kelly had been less than reticent in her devotion to Luke Kendall. She had managed to pop up wherever he was, and he didn't seem to mind. Or maybe he just didn't notice. Luke had taken his retinue of feminine admirers for granted, while Matt . . . Kelly remembered the wry grin that used to light up Matt's face whenever he had spotted her trailing after Luke. With grace and good humor, Matt had accepted the fact that his twin brother would probably always be subjected to an absurd degree of adulation.

Kelly wondered if Luke's legendary heroism had ever bothered Matt. He didn't act as if it did; he had never displayed any jealousy over Luke's popularity. And Matt had had his own fans, Kelly recalled. Jessie Ballinger, for example. Rather than keep a whole string of girls dangling as Luke had done, he'd dated one at a time, and had quietly befriended Luke's castoffs, too.

With the wisdom of her thirty years, Kelly asked herself what it was about Luke John that could have dazzled her so. Had it been his glib flirtatious tongue, his panache, his talent for monopolizing center stage? He wasn't any better looking than Matt, and he was a whole lot less reliable. Friend or no friend, Kelly couldn't imagine Luke extending himself for her, or for *anyone*, as Matt had done. That was the intrinsic difference in the two men. Probably it had always been, only Kelly had needed a few years to grow up in order to appreciate that difference.

That was her main reason for coming home. Not because of Matt, but because her values had changed.

Well, her style had changed, too. She no longer made a practice of shamelessly chasing after the object of her affections as she had when she was fifteen. Five years of portraying Lucia St. Claire had taught her a little about men, and now might be a good time to start applying that knowledge.

Yesterday she had received the impression that Matt was hesitant about getting involved romantically. Not totally dead set against it, she thought as she remembered the high-voltage energy behind his welcome-home embrace last night, but hesitant nevertheless. Perhaps it might be prudent at this point for Kelly to exercise a little restraint in her friendship with him.

Okay, she wouldn't pay a visit to the Kendalls quite this soon. She would thank Rita via the telephone. Much as she might like to see all the Kendalls in person, she'd rather not risk running into Matt. It wouldn't do for him to think she was hotly pursuing him.

Once she made up her mind about that, Kelly didn't linger in the bathtub. There were too many things to do around the house. She dressed in jeans and a sweater and headed for her old bedroom, where Matt had stashed her luggage.

The virtual mountain of boxes and suitcases would have daunted anyone else, but Kelly chose to think of it as a challenge. She had to figure a way to fit all those clothes into distinctly limited storage space. Deciding to move into her parents' bedroom on a permanent basis, she hung her absolutely essential garments in that empty closet. Old favorites that she seldom wore, she put in the closet in the bedroom of her childhood. That left an enormous pile of clothes on the bed, mostly party dresses that Kelly neither wanted nor had any use for in Weatherford.

She had an impulse to carry the stack out to the trash barrel and burn everything in a gesture symbolizing the end of her career. Before she could do so, the phone rang. It was a friend of her mother's, calling to see whether Kelly was recovering as well as Dr. Matt reported and asking if there was anything she needed.

By the time she had assured the lady that she was fine, Kelly's practical nature reared its head, and she had second thoughts about destroying perfectly good clothes. When the phone rang again, she gave the colorful heap of silks and satins a rueful look and granted them a reprieve.

Despite an extraordinary number of telephone calls from old friends and neighbors, Kelly managed to unpack and put away the contents of most of the boxes she'd brought from L.A. As she worked, she surveyed the house with a critical eye and realized that she didn't want to change very much about it. The delicate floral wallpaper in the bedrooms and bathroom and the solid colors in the living room and kitchen had worn well over the years. With a change of decorative accessories and several new pieces of furniture, she could achieve the cheerful country look she loved.

To start, she took down all the pictures and replaced them with pieces from her own collection of paintings by primitive American artists. At strategic points throughout the house, she placed framed works of needlepoint and cross-stitching that she had begun doing to pass the time on the set of *California Dreaming*. Not liking the drab brown curtains in the living room, she removed them and found that she much preferred the long, multipaned windows uncovered. Instantly the room appeared brighter despite the cloudiness of the December sky outside.

One of these days, she decided, she would go to Fort Worth and purchase a rug for the living room, a couple of lamps and a new sofa.

When at midafternoon she heard a knock on the front door, Kelly experienced a fleeting hope that it might be Matthew. Instead, she opened the door to a petite beauty with short blond curls and dark eyes.

"Jenny!" Kelly whooped in delighted surprise, throwing her arms around the slightly older version of Lisa Kendall. "It's so good to see you!" Releasing her, she peered out at the brown station wagon parked next to Kelly's BMW. "Didn't you bring Bill and the kids?"

"They're at Mom and Dad's, sleeping off Sunday dinner. When Matt said it was okay for you to have company, I sneaked out to see what you're up to."

"So my doctor's releasing me, hmm?" Kelly ushered her in out of the cold. "He must have let it slip to Millie. That would explain all the telephone calls I've been getting. People I haven't heard from in years have called to see how I'm feeling. It's amazing."

"What's really amazing is that everyone waited two days to call."

"I understand Matt had something to do with that." She tried to sound offhand. "Is he taking a nap, too?"

Jenny took off her jacket and dropped it onto the sofa. "Matt's still at the hospital. I talked to him when he called to apologize for missing dinner. Again. Matt misses a lot of meals."

For the next two hours the friends sat across from each other at the round table in the kitchen, drinking coffee and catching up on recent happenings.

"I can't believe you're really moving back here, Kelly," Jenny said for the fifth time.

"Why not? I told you in my last letter that I planned to."

"Yes, but I didn't take you seriously." Jenny shook her head in puzzlement. "You've been so successful on television. Why would you want to give all that up?"

"Maybe I'm ready to try my hand at something else."

"Like what?"

"Oh, I don't know." Kelly's eyes shone with mischief. "When I was a kid, I had a hankering to work at the Dairy Bar."

"Sure," Jenny scoffed. "I can just see you now, slaving away for minimum wage."

"Money's not an issue, thank goodness. If it makes you feel any better, I had excellent financial advice and invested well over the past five years. It just might be fun to spend my time making banana splits and hot fudge sundaes all day long."

"It would certainly make for a change, at any rate. Imagine Lucia St. Claire parading around in one of those frilly aprons and a hair net."

"A hair net?" Suddenly looking skeptical, Kelly ran one hand through her unrestrained coppery tresses. "On second thought, I'd better reconsider my future plans."

"And go back to Hollywood?"

"No. I'll just have to come up with another career."

"I'm glad to see you, Kelly, but I never thought you'd voluntarily give up the excitement of starring in *California Dreaming* to come back to Weatherford. You used to say this place stifled you."

"I used to say a lot of things that I don't say anymore. Do you remember the time I made a solemn vow that I was never going to get married?"

Laughing, Jenny nodded. "At the time you were furious with Luke for some reason or another." Her expression changed. "Do you mean to say marriage is next on your agenda?"

Kelly hastened to quell the gleam in her friend's eyes. "Not at all! I only gave that as an example of my erratic nature. Although you make a good case for marriage and a family. Motherhood obviously agrees with you."

Once flighty and boy-crazy, Jenny had matured into a serene woman who exhibited tremendous satisfaction with her life.

"Thanks, but I envy you your freedom."

Kelly pooh-poohed that idea. "You know darn well you don't envy me a thing. You've never for a minute regretted marrying Bill."

"You're right," Jenny said with a grin. "But I've gotta hand it to you. You and my brother do lead interesting lives. I still get a vicarious thrill every time I turn on the television and see you or Luke John."

"Rita told me how proud she is when the whole family gets together to go see one of Luke's movies in Fort Worth."

Jenny's smile faded as she stared down at the cup of coffee she held between both palms. "Did she tell you Matt won't go with us? I don't think he's ever seen one of Luke's movies."

"You're kidding." Kelly looked closely at Jenny. "Aren't you? Why wouldn't he go?"

"I have no idea. He just always has some excuse why he can't go with us." She glanced up, her eyes troubled. "Another thing . . . I've noticed that every time the radio station plays one of Luke John's songs, Matt either leaves the room or turns it off."

"That doesn't sound like Matt," Kelly said, then remembered the way he had tried to change the station the day before when she was listening to Lisa's radio. "Do you think he's jealous?"

"It makes me wonder." In an angry gesture, Jenny struck the table with her fist. "Darn it, Kelly, I know that's not true! I know Matt has never begrudged Luke his success. He's never wanted to be famous himself. All he's ever wanted is to be the best doctor around."

"Well, he's accomplished that, all right." Kelly spoke with conviction despite her uneasy feelings. "I can't believe how much of himself he gives to people. There's no comparison between his career and Luke John's. Or mine."

Jenny gave her a searching look. "Now *that's* something you wouldn't have said a few years ago. You used to adore my brother."

"I still do."

"Which one?"

"Both of them."

"Matt? Is it Matt who interests you now?"

"I told you, Matt's incredible," Kelly said evasively.

"You really think he contributes more to society than Luke?"

"Look, Jenny, I don't intend to get into a philosophical debate over the relative value of entertainment versus medicine."

"Of course not. Just answer this: Do you still feel the same way about Luke that you did when we were younger?"

Kelly hesitated. "I've changed. We've all changed."

"I know." Jenny waved a hand impatiently. "What I want to know is, are you still in love with him?"

"What I felt for Luke was never love. It was more like hero worship."

"I see. Well, are you in love with someone else?"

"No."

"What about that guy you dated from the show—Doug Barron?"

"No way. He wrote me off when I left Hollywood." When Jenny broke into a huge smile, Kelly developed a couple of serious misgivings. "Hey, hold it. You're acting just like you used to when you were plotting to trick Luke into taking me out. It never worked, in case you've forgotten.'

Jenny's smile broadened.

Kelly slammed her mug down and sloshed coffee all over the table. "Oh, no, you don't, Jenny Kendall! I'm not interested in Luke John anymore."

"Who said anything about Luke?"

"Well, then, who . . . ?"

Jenny got up and plucked the dishcloth out of the sink, proceeding to calmly mop up Kelly's mess.

"Jenny, damn it, who?"

Matt's sister carried the dripping cloth back to the sink and rinsed it out, then folded it carefully and spread it over the rim, smiling mysteriously all the while.

Kelly scowled. "You'd better not be thinking of fixing me up with Matt."

Jenny leaned against the counter and looked innocently at Kelly.

"I mean it, Jenny! I won't let you test your matchmaking skills on Matt and me. It was one thing when we were teenagers, but I absolutely refuse to go along with you now. Not with Matt."

Folding her arms on her chest, Jenny assumed a questioning pose.

"It just wouldn't work!" Kelly stormed. "Matt's not interested in getting involved with a woman. You're the one who's told me that a hundred times in the past seven years, for heaven's sake!"

Jenny nodded. "I told you that, all right."

"Every time you write, you mention something about Matt still being in mourning for Meredith. Your mother told me just yesterday that she doesn't think he'll ever fall in love again."

"We all worry about Matt."

"Well, then, don't push it. There's no point in trying to force him into a relationship he doesn't want."

"I agree," Jenny murmured to Kelly's astonishment.

"You do?"

"Certainly. He's just like that man in Luke John's new song. I'm afraid he'll go to his grave loving Meredith."

Kelly's heart plunged to her toes at Jenny's matter-of-fact statement, nor did her next words make Kelly feel any better.

"Besides, even if Matt wasn't hopelessly hung up on a ghost, I wouldn't make the mistake of trying to fix you two up."

"You . . . wouldn't?"

"Good grief, no. I'm aware that you and Matt would never hit it off."

We do too hit it off, Kelly protested silently, recalling in vivid detail the sensual fire of Matt's kisses scorching her lips and searing the tender curve of her throat.

Flushing, she said, "No, of course we wouldn't."

"Of course not! You're more like his sister—"

I don't feel like his sister, she thought rebelliously.

"—and I know you think of Matt as a brother."

"Oh . . . sure."

"No, you're all wrong for each other. Matt's not your type at all." When Kelly didn't say anything, Jenny asked, "Is he?"

"No," she muttered.

"Because you had plenty of opportunity to vamp him back in high school if you'd been interested, but you couldn't see anyone but Luke John."

Don't remind me, Kelly thought, staring gloomily at the tabletop. Had she really missed her chance with Matt? She glanced up in time to see a wicked, plotting expression on Jenny's face. That look made her suspicious. "Okay, if it's not Matt you're trying to foist on me, who is it?"

"'Foist' on you? Really, Kelly! We're friends. I wouldn't do that to you. I have only your best interest at heart."

"*Who?*" Kelly shouted.

Jenny smiled angelically. "Homer Whetsel."

"Homer Whetsel? *Not* the Homer Whetsel in my graduating class in school!"

"The very one."

Kelly counted to ten slowly. "Jenny Kendall, I'm going to forget you started this."

"But, Kelly, Homer's very nice. He owns a bowling alley."

"Homer chewed tobacco in high school!"

"Come to think of it, he still does. But he really is a pretty good catch. If you could talk him into dieting and bathing once in a while, he wouldn't be half bad."

Kelly glared at Jenny. "Is Homer Whetsel the only bachelor in town?"

"No, but I figured you'd want to start at the top."

"The top! Homer ranked in the lower one percentile when we were eighteen years old, and from the way you describe him he hasn't improved with age."

"Okay, okay, calm down," Jenny soothed her. "I'll tell you what. You need to look over the available male population and decide for yourself which one you'd like to go out with."

"Which *one*?" Kelly asked dryly.

"Well, one or two. Let's not get our hopes up. I mean, if you don't like Homer, you may prove difficult to please. Anyway, I have the perfect place in mind for you to start looking. Keep your calendar clear for Tuesday night."

"What's happening Tuesday night?"

"You'll see."

"Will Homer be there?"

"Honestly, Kelly, I was just kidding about Homer." Kelly was not amused.

6

ICY RAIN PELTED the windshield of the station wagon as it plowed through the darkness. Leaning forward and keeping one hand on the steering wheel to drive, Jenny used a paper napkin to wipe clear a circle on the fogged-over glass. Streetlights and illuminated windows in houses that they passed were barely visible through the downpour. There seemed to be no other traffic on the streets.

"I see no one else was crazy enough to go out in this weather," Kelly remarked. "Was it absolutely necessary to drag me along, wherever it is you're going?"

"Need I remind you that we're going on your account?" Jenny asked. "*I'm* not looking for a husband."

"Neither am I."

In the dim light of the dashboard, Jenny smiled to herself but didn't argue with Kelly.

Kelly bit back a sharp request for Jenny to stop looking so smug and instead said calmly, "Would you mind telling me where we're going?"

"Don't you recognize this part of town? It hasn't changed that much since you moved away."

Kelly squinted out at the obscure scenery. "This is the route we used to take on our way to school every morning, isn't it?" At Jenny's nod, she raised an eyebrow. "We're going to the high school? What on earth for?"

"To watch a basketball game."

"Let me guess: I get my pick of the guys on the team."

Jenny slanted her a speculative look and noted the dramatic gray cape she wore with high black boots. Even in the faint light of the car, Kelly looked smashing. "Oh, I imagine you can take your pick, at least of the players who aren't already spoken for."

"Wonderful," Kelly drawled. "I'm just crazy about high school boys."

"Honestly!" Jenny rolled her eyes. "Did I say this is a high school game we're going to see?"

Just then she swung the car off the street and into the parking lot, maneuvering as close as possible to the doors of the big gymnasium. All of the dozen or so other cars already parked seemed to have had the same idea and were clustered haphazardly against the curb.

Wasn't that Matt's Blazer over there? Kelly dropped her casual pose. "Just exactly who *is* playing?"

"I call them the 'Over-The-Hill Gang,' but the oldest is Wade Farnsworth. He just turned forty." Seeing Kelly's frown, she added, "Come on, Kel. It's just a bunch of guys who get together every week to have some fun and get in a little exercise."

"The cream of Weatherford's bachelor crop?"

"And a few old married men," her friend agreed dryly. "Bill plays forward."

Kelly didn't dare mention Matt. She knew he was in there playing, and she didn't want to admit she knew. Because then she'd feel obligated to protest, and maybe Jenny would take her home, even though she really did want to see him. He had called her Sunday evening to ask how she felt, but she hadn't heard from him since. It had been a long two days.

She cleared her throat. "Bill's on the team, huh? This I've gotta see."

They both got drenched on their mad dash from the car, prompting Jenny to suggest that they make a pit stop before proceeding any farther. In the rest room, Kelly took off her cape and hung it over a stall door, then gave her head a couple of brisk shakes to scatter the moisture she had collected.

"Phooey!" Jenny muttered, watching her. "You look better than ever. I look like a drowned rat."

"Actually, my pint-sized friend, you look more like a waterlogged kitten."

Jenny turned to a mirror to see if she needed to repair her makeup. "Nice outfit you're wearing," she said.

"Thanks." Kelly liked the gray miniplaid shirt and calf-length split skirt herself, perhaps because it made the most of her tall legginess. She faced another mirror and ran a wand of gloss over her lips, giving them a coppery-peach shine. Dropping the tube into her gray leather handbag, she retrieved her cape and headed for the door. "Let's go take a look at the Weatherford Wonders."

She strolled into the enormous, brightly lit gym as if she owned the place...as if she didn't have a crazy urge to scurry beneath the bleachers and hide so Matt Kendall wouldn't think she was chasing him.

But Kelly hadn't become Soap's Sexiest Meanie by letting her insecurities run her life. All those years onstage had polished her talent for pretending, and now she lifted her chin and pretended to be nonchalant. She pretended for all of sixty seconds before the atmosphere in the gym took her back so far in time that she couldn't pretend any longer.

She shut her eyes and became a high school sophomore once again, packed in among her friends high up in the stands, watching the Kangaroos down on the court in their blue-and-white uniforms playing for the district championship. The air was overheated, the crowd screaming, the bleachers groaning and creaking, the players running back and forth accompanied by the rhythmic thudding of the basketball on the wooden floor and the sharp sound of flesh slapping leather as the ball was tossed around. Luke John had been right in the middle of it all, playing center position and looking too magnificent to believe from the top of the grandstand.

Kelly opened her eyes, and the crowd disappeared. A handful of spectators sat in the second row up, while two teams of motley-clad players—not one under the age of thirty—occupied the court, their vigorous efforts punctuated by shouts and grunts. The air was redolent of perspiration and soap mixed with ten different after shave lotions. None of the uniforms matched, giving Kelly cause to wonder how the men knew who was on what team.

It was a fascinating game, drawn in vivid colors and exuding such masculine energy that Kelly's mouth curved into a smile of unconscious excitement. She watched the action on the floor for a moment, easily picking out Matt by his brilliant blond curls. With his long sun-bronzed arms and legs displayed in gray shorts and T-shirt, he resembled a golden Apollo more than an ordinary mortal. Something closely akin to liquid fire began simmering through her bloodstream, warming her, stealing her oxygen. She felt breathless and so full of awe that she couldn't seem to stop staring.

"Something wrong?" Jenny inquired blandly.

Kelly tried to sound reprimanding. "Matthew's here!"

But she heard the elation in her voice. Worse, Jenny must have heard it, too. Kelly forced her gaze away from the most beautiful male creature she'd ever laid eyes on and glared at his sister. "Darn you, Jenny Kendall, I *told* you I didn't want you to fix me up with him."

Jenny widened her eyes. "With Matt? Don't be silly, Kelly. I didn't bring you here to see him. Besides—" she cast a meaningful glance at the small audience, who had turned their collective attention from the game and were watching Kelly with unconcealed interest "—I see Matt already has one admirer here tonight. Come on, let's sit down."

As she followed Jenny to join the others on the bleachers, Kelly wondered which of the three young women Jenny had been referring to. All were attractive and friendly, and as Jenny introduced them Kelly saw that the one named Angela Guest was actually quite stunning, her long hair as blond and silky-looking as Matt's, her eyes a deep violet. Kelly fervently hoped that she had a husband out there playing basketball. But Angela held a pair of gray sweatpants on her lap in an undeniably possessive way, and when she crossed her legs the pants shifted and allowed Kelly a glimpse of a familiar jacket underneath. Matt's jacket. Jenny informed her brightly that Angela was Matt's receptionist.

The women, as well as the two young men, questioned Kelly briefly about her career, and then seemed to accept her as one of them, which suited her just fine. She only wanted to watch the game and try to regain control of her stormy emotions.

She *couldn't* be jealous. Angela might have cause to be possessive of Matt Kendall, but Kelly West certainly didn't. She had no claim on him except the powerful ties of friendship that reached back to their childhood. And perhaps Matt didn't feel the bond as strongly as she did.

Look at him out there, she thought irritably. He knew Angela was watching him. Hunched over with his arms outspread, he guarded an opponent who had the ball. When the other player moved, Matt moved, sticking to him tenaciously, determined to get the ball away. Muscles bunched in his well-shaped legs as he crouched and ran. Sweat dripped down his temples to his chin, giving his face a healthy sheen. His brown eyes snapped with life, and his sensuous mouth broke into a grin of devilish enjoyment.

Oh, yes, he knew, and he was giving his pretty fan quite a show. With a finesse that would have impressed Kareem Abdul-Jabbar, Matt snatched the basketball away from his prey, spun around and began dribbling to the other end of the court, weaving in and out of the rest of the players, deftly avoiding his pursuers. Because none of his teammates got in the clear, he didn't pass off but charged in for the shot himself, leaping and twisting in midair to plunk the ball neatly into the basket. He landed on his feet with both arms raised high in triumph, grinning at the rowdy cheers his achievement earned. As he ran back down the court, Kelly saw him veer over to Bill Lewis and speak to him, then nod toward the sideline, his grin still in place. Oh, yes, Matt knew about Angela, all right.

Jenny leaned closer to Kelly. "See anyone interesting?" she whispered.

All Kelly could see was a blond sexpot scrambling to regain possession of the ball. "Mmmm . . ." she said, as if she was really considering the question.

"The tall dark one with the incredible shoulders is Bob Willoughby. He's in construction."

The only incredible shoulders she had noticed were Matt's, but Kelly at least made an effort to figure out which one Jenny was talking about. "Oh, him," she said indifferently. "I don't like his nose."

"Really? I think he's got an interesting nose."

"So *you* date him." She found Matt again and discovered that his nose was perfect.

After a minute, Jenny elbowed her again. "Look at the one in the number sixty-seven sweatshirt. That's Bart Breedlove, the high school tennis coach. His divorce was final last month, and rumor has it he has to fight off the women with a stick."

Kelly narrowed her gaze on the man in question and wrinkled her nose. "I don't believe it."

Jenny giggled. "Neither do I. But he is sort of cute, don't you think? In a little-boy way? I mean, red hair and freckles . . ."

"He's okay." Kelly shrugged and went back to studying Matt. *His* skin was smooth and evenly tanned without a single blemish . . . except for that scar on his temple, and he'd probably got that while rescuing a kitten stranded atop the windmill.

"Eureka!" Jenny forgot to keep her voice down. When Angela gave her an expectant look, she waggled her fingers and grinned sheepishly. "Wade Farnsworth," she whispered to Kelly, nodding at the elegantly slender player in the designer jogging suit. "He's a lawyer."

That much Kelly remembered. The son of a local banker, he had already opened his law practice in Weatherford when Kelly had graduated from high school. She looked him over now, duly noting his perfectly styled brown hair and his coordinated appearance.

"Not my type."

Jenny made a show of throwing up her hands and groaning. "You're hopeless, Kelly! What am I supposed to do—import men for you?"

"You don't have to do anything. I've only been home four days, and part of that time I was sick in bed. For the love of heaven, Jenny, give me a chance."

"Yeah, Jenny, give the lady a chance."

Kelly's heart jumped into her throat at Matt's soft-spoken echo. She had been so involved in her tirade that she hadn't noticed the abrupt breakup of the game nor Matt's pantherish approach. Flustered, she watched him sprawl out on the bench just below her, lean his head back against the hard bleachers and shut his eyes. Most of the other players had likewise found a spot to collapse, and Jenny was in the process of vanishing out the door with Bill.

"Hi, Kelly."

Looking down at his broad chest, she swallowed hard. "Hi, Matthew."

"What is Jenny supposed to give you a chance to do?"

Her furtive eyes roamed the length of his arms and legs, and her fingertips itched to explore the dusting of golden hair on olive skin. Just look at him! Just imagine what his bare muscular limbs must feel like...damp, hot, powerful, pulsing with life. Imagine stretching out beside him there and reaching up to finger his silky hair. Imagine...no, don't imagine that here!

"I just told her I can find my own husband," Kelly answered without thinking.

Dark eyes popped wide open in surprise. "What?"

Oh, dear. She definitely hadn't meant to say *that*. "Forget it," she said quickly, giving him a bright smile. "Was I ever surprised to see you here tonight! I had no idea you still played basketball." That, she hoped, would convince him she didn't have designs on him.

He grinned up at her and reached out to trace a fingertip along her sleeve. In response, a heart-melting shiver danced through her. "If you were dressed a little more appropriately, I'd get you out on the court and see if *you* can still play."

His husky voice thrilled her. "We used to have fun, didn't we? I remember shooting baskets out by your dad's barn," she said. "You and me and Luke John—"

Some of the warmth left his velvet brown eyes at that, and he sat up and looked around, giving her no chance to finish. "Has anyone seen my sweatpants?" he asked above the murmur of nearby conversations.

Angela stood and brought over Matt's clothes, reaching past Kelly to hand them to him without a word.

"Thanks, Angel." Matt sent her an absent smile, beginning at once to pull on his pants.

The expression on the other woman's face smote Kelly with sympathy, so that for the moment she forgot the way Matt had cut her off in midsentence. Furthermore, it convinced her that Matt must be unaware of Angela's feelings for him. He seemed as oblivious to her as Luke John had been to Kelly all those years, and that could hurt badly.

Kelly also noticed, blended in with her compassion for Angela, heady swirls of relief that Matt Kendall wasn't involved with the lovely blonde. It made her want to throw her arms around his neck and proceed recklessly from there.

Instead, she waved at his sweatpants. "Do you have to wear those things?"

One leg in and one out, he paused and lifted an eyebrow at her quizzically.

"You have sexy legs." Somehow she kept a perfectly straight face while leering at the firmly muscled thigh that almost touched hers. "It's a shame to cover them up."

After a brief hesitation, he smiled and stuck his foot into the pant leg. "Thanks, but I don't really care to risk frostbite just to give you a thrill."

Kelly snapped her fingers. "Oh, well. Can't blame me for trying."

He stood and pulled the stretchy waistband into place around his trim middle, then reached for his jacket, all the time eyeing Kelly as if trying to figure her out. Finally he shook his head and nodded toward the loud discussion in progress down on the court. "The guys are meeting at the Dairy Bar for hamburgers. Want to come with me?"

She wanted to. Oh, boy, did she ever want to! But she cautioned herself not to act too eager.

Glancing around, she said doubtfully, "I don't know, Matt. I came with Jenny."

"If I know my sister, she's halfway home by now. Bill rode over with me, but he's not here now, as you can see. You've been deserted."

"Well, darn her hide!"

It was Matt's turn to look solemn. "I don't imagine you feel much like a six-mile hike in the rain, do you?"

"I'll kill her!"

"Seems to me I recall you making that same threat a time or two back in our younger days." He put on his jacket. "How about that hamburger?"

She hesitated. "With a Cherry Coke?"

"And fried onion rings."

She heaved an exaggerated sigh. "You talked me into it."

THE RAIN STOPPED as Matt drove Kelly home. With his eyes on the road, he listened to Kelly singing along to an old top-forties hit on the radio, her enthusiastic "da-do-ron-rons" accompanied by the hissing of wet pavement beneath the tires. When the tune ended, he glanced over at her and said what he'd been thinking all evening. "You made a helluva fine recovery from that flu bug, Kelly."

"Recovery?" She flung her hand across her forehead. "Who's recovered? I think I'm about to suffer a serious relapse." *And you, Dr. Matt, may have to spend another night with me . . . with decidedly different results from the last time.*

Oh, no, you don't! he swore silently. *You're not my patient anymore. I'm about to make that official.*

"Sorry. After the way you ate tonight, I have no choice but to pronounce you cured."

Lowering her arm, she sniffed. "Rather ungallant of you to notice my gluttony." Hopefully she added, "I don't guess you'd buy it if I told you I passed most of my food under the table to a small dog with a very large appetite?"

"Not for a minute."

"I didn't think you would." She giggled. "I really did pig out, didn't I?"

They had turned off the highway and were bouncing along the lane that led to her house. The song that had just started playing sounded like one of Luke John's, but before Kelly could be sure Matt reached for the radio knob and snapped it off. "I'd better take the Fifth on that question," he said. "Anyway, I think you can afford to put on a few pounds."

"You think I'm too skinny?"

"Let me put it this way: If you were my patient, I'd start you on a weight-gain program tomorrow."

If she were his patient? Kelly's eyebrows rose, but she merely said, "I could handle that. I love to eat."

"I got that impression tonight. It's been a long time since I watched anybody eat with such gusto."

She sighed happily. "Lord, I'd forgotten just how good hamburgers can be! I'm here to tell you, they don't make 'em like that in Hollywood."

He pulled the Blazer to a stop and killed the engine, shutting off the headlights and plunging the interior into total darkness. "Then you're not mad at Jenny for running out on you?"

Feeling replete and daring, Kelly stretched, letting one hand brush Matt's shoulder, then settle there. Even through the thickness of his corduroy jacket and T-shirt, she recognized the hard power of his muscles. A delicious warmth inched through her, and a tightness gripped her throat. "No, I'm not mad. You weren't really surprised when she left, were you?"

She felt rather than saw his shrug in the dimness. "It didn't take a lot of smarts to anticipate her sneaky move. She obviously wanted me to give you a ride home. Miss Fix-it thinks she can make the two of us fall in love."

Kelly thought she detected a note of displeasure in his voice. She turned to face him on the seat. "Matt, I'm sorry."

"Why should you be sorry?"

"Because I know you hate being maneuvered into something that might be construed as a date. I'm sure you'd rather everyone just left you alone to decide for yourself if and when you ever feel like getting involved with a woman again. And heaven knows that's your right. But you have to understand that Jenny only interferes because she cares about you so much."

"I'm aware of that."

"She just wants you to be happy. And to Jenny, being happy means being married."

"I know."

"Well, then, don't hold her romantic scheming against her. She has good intentions."

"I'm not holding anything against Jenny."

Matt captured the hand that still rested on his shoulder, laced his fingers through Kelly's and squeezed. A brilliant flash of pleasure lanced through her, and her pulse quickened.

"I don't allow myself to be maneuvered into dates," he was saying in a low, calm voice. "I'm right where I want to be. What about you?"

His unexpected revelation made it impossible for her to be less than honest with him. "I can't think of any place I'd rather be, or anyone I'd rather be with."

Matt's chest constricted, and his throat ached with intense longing. He wanted to believe she meant what she said. He wanted to forget she had ever hero-worshiped Luke to the point that she patterned her life after his. And why shouldn't he forget it? That was the past; this was now. Kelly had put Hollywood behind her and had come back home to Weatherford. It had been her choice, which surely said something about her feelings, or lack of them, for Luke.

He took a deep breath and pressed his palm to her smooth cheek, then leaned forward and covered her mouth with his in a brief but potent kiss. At the touch of his lips, both silky and provocatively rough, a sweet, hot joy bubbled up inside her. He tasted of french fries and Pepsi Cola and excitement. But he withdrew much too soon, leaving her appetite whetted and her soul reaching toward his virile warmth . . . a warmth that retreated with alarming speed.

No, she thought rebelliously. *You can't pull that on me again!*

But already he was opening the door and getting out, saying, "I hope you left your heat turned up," and going around to help her out of the car.

Fast and furiously her mind processed plans of action and then rejected them as he walked her up to the porch. *Swoon. Fake a heart attack. Confess that you're suffering from the heartbreak of psoriasis. Anything to keep him here! Throw your arms around his waist and attach yourself so securely to his body that you'll have to be surgically removed. Or . . . this might be a good time for that mild attack of insanity you've been saving up for.*

"You are coming in, aren't you," she said, not really asking. She unlocked the door and stepped inside, looking expectantly at Matt, who hesitated on the threshold.

"It's pretty late. I'd like to but—"

"You have to." She took his hand, and he allowed himself to be drawn in out of the cold night.

"Why do I have to?"

"Because. Because you...you have to check for burglars," she blurted, pleased with her cleverness. "You know, look in the closets and under the beds. All the usual places."

"You're afraid of burglars?" He looked skeptical.

"Terrified," she lied blithely. She shut the front door, hung her cape on the coatrack, then held out her hand and tapped her foot until he relinquished his jacket to the same fate. She smiled up at him. "Don't forget the shower."

He assumed an ironic expression. "You want me to take a shower? I thought that was Willoughby I was smelling all evening."

Kelly narrowed her eyes and looked him up and down, thinking that this might be a splendid opportunity to discover if coeducational bathing was all it was cracked up to be. On second thought, better not suggest it. "Everybody knows the shower is a classic hiding place for psychos, Matthew," she explained patiently. "While you're looking, I'll go plug in the coffeepot."

She was watching the coffee begin to perk when she heard him enter the kitchen. He approached her from behind and slid his hands around her waist, coming close enough that the gently rounded curve of her bottom nestled against his pelvis. Realizing with a shock of electric awareness just what portion of his anatomy touched her so intimately, she shut her eyes and surrendered herself to a heavenly lassitude. Indescribably lovely sensations began radiating out from the fount of her femininity, charging her with lazy pleasure. Even if she could have moved, she wouldn't have, because to move would have been to risk disturbing the delicate balance of this contact. Matt was touching her, yet he wasn't really *doing* anything, and it was a torture of the most enjoyable kind.

After a minute, his arms tightened, and he bent his head to kiss her just below her earlobe. "The coast is clear," he murmured against her throat.

She tried to ask what he was talking about and only managed to make a gurgling sound.

"No psychos anywhere," he assured her, nuzzling down her neck into the open collar of her blouse.

"Thanks for . . . for checking," she gasped as his lips happened upon the swelling tops of her breasts and began tasting.

"Mmmm . . . I'm glad I could calm your fears."

Calm her? She felt anything but calm, especially when he straightened up and turned her around to face him, his brown eyes concentrated on the gap where her top button had come undone. With deft fingers, he unfastened several more and spread the material apart, then lowered his mouth to the creamy mounds that seemed to invite his exploration. The lacy cups of her bra covered very little skin above the nipples and did nothing at all to stop his adventuresome tongue.

Kelly arched her back and moaned, and Matt quickly grasped her derriere with both hands and pressed her firmly to him. The feel of his hard fullness straining against the front of his stretchy sweatpants, vigorously informing her of his arousal, completely wiped out any comment she might have intended to make. She plunged her fingers into the silky silver-gold curls at her breast and clutched his head to her, trying not to pant too obviously.

He nibbled his way from one side to the other and back again, his mouth hot and magic. Soon she was hot all over too, and he was burning with fevered desire.

With supreme effort he lifted his head. "I think I'd better pass on the coffee, Kelly."

She stared dazedly at the sensuous line of his lower lip and imagined what it would feel like branding the soft plane of her stomach. "Me, too," she said, shivering.

"I've got to go." But he spoke reluctantly and made no move to release her.

Lowering her lashes to hide the alarm that flared in her eyes, she focused on the T-shirt covering his muscular chest. "Are you sure you have to?"

"I'm sure I'd better."

"But do you want to?"

"Do I want to go?" He laughed shortly, his strong brown throat contracting jerkily as he swallowed. "No, that's not what I want at all."

"What *do* you want?"

He shuddered convulsively. "What I want—Oh, Kelly, if the AMA knew what I've been wanting to do to you for the past four days, they'd take away my stethoscope!"

The husky anguish in his voice prompted her to look up into his face, where she saw a wide array of emotions, hunger competing with tender amusement for dominance.

She wrapped her arms around his waist. "Why, Matt?"

"Because, dammit! Because I took an oath not to—"

"Not to make love?"

He grimaced at her wry question. "Not with one of my patients."

At this point she guessed the proper thing to do would be to drop the subject and go on to something a little less brazen. She remained silent a moment, wondering whether to be proper or honest. "Didn't you tell me I'm all cured?" At his nod she added, "And if I catch pneumonia tomorrow, what would you have me do?"

"I would have you not get sick again...*ever*." A tiny candle flame flickered to life in those warm, dark eyes, and he almost smiled. "But if you do, I'd have you call Dr. Slater. I trust her to take good care of you."

"If you trust her, then so do I. So am I one of your patients now?"

His left hand released her tush long enough for him to consult his wristwatch. "Not for the last half hour." He sounded very satisfied with that fact.

Kelly tipped her head back. "Mm-hmm. Now you were saying something about what you want...."

Matt was trapped, bewitched, enchanted by those green cat's eyes. He reached up a hand and stroked her hair, his trembling fingers weaving into the coppery strands. "Kelly, I want you," he said, his voice hoarse, his heart pounding. Because he feared she didn't reciprocate the feeling, he hastened to add, "You don't have to remind me I shouldn't feel this way about you. I've been telling myself that ever since you came back to town. Even if you're not my patient anymore, you're one of my best friends, Kelly, and good friends aren't supposed to entertain erotic fantasies about each other." He slowly removed his hand from her hair. "If you'll just give me a chance, I'll get my lust under control." Six months and a thousand cold showers should do the trick.

"I hope not!"

He blinked, certain he had misunderstood. "What?"

"I have no complaints about your lust, Matt. You've starred in a few of my own fantasies."

His crooked grin captivated her. "You sure you didn't get me confused with Luke John?"

"Positive. I especially like one fantasy that I keep having. We're standing here in the kitchen, like this." She put her hands on his shoulders as if to adjust his position. "And I kiss you...like this." Leaning forward, she traced her tongue along the outline of his lips to the corner, then licked delicately. She knew from his sudden taut inhalation that he found the gesture tormenting. "And then," she purred against his mouth, "you pick me up and take me to the bedroom...."

He scooped her up into his arms and held her close to his pounding heart. "Like this?"

"Exactly."

He carried her through the house and didn't stop until he reached her bed. "Then what do I do?"

"Put me down."

"And then?"

Her hands clung to his neck, her fingers playing with a lock of his soft blond hair. "What do you think?"

She had never known his eyes could glow with such brilliance. "Can I show you?" he asked.

"Please do!"

7

KELLY LAY ON HER BACK in the middle of the bed where Matt had placed her. The smile curving her mouth was secretive and more than just a bit anticipatory as she watched him switch the light off and the lamp on. Turning, he sat down beside her.

"Now I do this." And he proceeded to unfasten the last of her buttons and gently tug the blouse up out of the waistband of her skirt, then spread the two sides to expose her flesh.

Was she too thin? Kelly waited anxiously for his reaction.

His expression solemn, his lashes downcast, Matt continued undressing her in silence until she lay before him in all her natural glory... albeit not feeling very glorious. She *was* skinny, darn it! He probably thought she resembled an emaciated scarecrow. All that wretched dieting had ruined her figure. Kelly felt a rash of gooseflesh break out all over her and wished she could cover herself.

Matt stared for a full minute before he lifted his head and let her see the look in his eyes—the look of a man gazing at a woman he considers beautiful. His expression was totally appreciative, and it warmed away the chills that had begun to invade Kelly's heart.

"Now this." Slowly his head came down, and he buried his nose between her full breasts and took a deep breath. "Mmmm . . . delicious!"

Hundreds of tiny shock waves rippled over Kelly's nerve endings, set off by the touch of his face against her, so that she almost didn't hear his whispered pronouncement.

"What's delicious?" she gasped when his words finally registered.

"The way you smell." He spoke against her ribs, his breath tickling. The tip of his tongue pressed his brand on her skin, hot and wet and sensually captivating. "The way you taste."

Before she could respond his hands grasped her waist, and his thumbs began stroking in circles of such vivid, concentrated feeling that her voice deserted her. Kelly lay in stunned silence as his hands beguiled, as he drew his mouth down, his tongue searing an erotic path with excruciating tenderness from her breastbone to her belly. At her navel he stopped, and the point of his tongue snaked out to bathe the tiny crevice thoroughly and without haste.

The shock waves were growing stronger by the second. Transfixed with wonder, Kelly focused on the broad span of shoulders and the crown of silver-gold curls above her. As the increasingly urgent tremors shook her, Matt nuzzled the smooth surface of her stomach, his lips evoking a need such as she had never known before. The torture was blissful and unbearable.

"Matt!"

His name emerged from her paralyzed throat as a squeak, and at the sound he raised his head. His eyes were foggy, lost in an ancient dream. "Hmmm?"

"Is this *your* fantasy—" she swallowed with difficulty "—or mine?"

Blinking, he felt a guilty flush suffuse his face. "Uh...ours?" His hands tightened on her slender waist. "Am I doing something wrong?"

She shook her head and licked her lips. "You're doing everything right. That's the problem."

Matt straightened, frowning, and would have released her if she hadn't caught his hands and held them where they were. "It's a problem? I don't understand."

"Don't ask questions, Matthew," she ordered him softly, sitting up to face him. "Trust me."

Still frowning, he said, "But how can it be a prob—"

Abruptly she leaned forward to put a fingertip to his lips and shivered when her nipples encountered the unyielding hardness of his chest. "I want to help, Matt. In my fantasy, I get in on the fun parts, too. Like this."

His puzzled look changed to one of surprised comprehension as Kelly caught the hem of his gray T-shirt and started jerking it up and off him. He raised his arms in automatic cooperation, and by the time his head emerged and she tossed the shirt aside, a grin of delight had split his face. When she laid her palm flat against the supple wall of his chest and tweaked a silky gold tuft of hair, his smile broadened. "I think I like your fantasy, Kelly."

"Oh, Matthew, this is just the beginning!"

Emitting a low growl of pleasure, he flicked a finger at his sweatpants. "Don't forget these. I guess you'll get rid of them next?"

"Absolutely." She used one knee to push him off the bed and then scrambled after him. "If you had only followed my advice at the gym, you could have saved us a good ten seconds here." It gave her enormous pleasure to insert her thumbs into the waist of his pants and pull them down his splendid brown legs, although the gesture might have been more satisfying if he hadn't still been wearing his gym shorts and tennis shoes.

Matt forgot the chilling weather outside and agreed fervently that for the sake of time, he really should have left off the pants. When the elastic band at his ankle got stuck around his left shoe and it began to look as if the entire tangle of unwanted clothing would remain shackled to his foot the rest of the night, he vowed never to wear pants again. What if she grew tired of the delay and sent him packing?

The sight of Kelly West, stark naked and sexy as sin, down on her hands and knees yanking at Matt's obstinate pant leg, interrupted his gloomy thoughts.

"Any idiot knows you take off your shoes first, *then* your pants," she grumbled under her breath, and Matt wondered just which idiot she blamed for the mishap. She looked so lithe and huggable, he wanted to curl up with her—right there on the floor would suit him just fine.

Suddenly the sweatpants pulled free, and Kelly went tumbling backward, landing on her bottom with a thud.

"Kelly!" he shouted, and launched himself off the edge of the bed where he'd been sitting with his foot outstretched. Kneeling beside her, he stared apprehensively at the peculiar expression on her face. "Kelly, are you okay?"

Kelly was fine, despite the undignified manner in which she'd just taken her seat. She eyed Matt silently while her thoughts raced. Mercy, he was fantastic . . . a perfect bronze Adonis in gym shorts. The trouble was, he had concern and chagrin etched all over his hand-some face. Where was the raw desire that had been there moments ago? It would take a miracle to light *that* fire again. Between the two of them, they'd managed to hopelessly complicate what had promised to be a simple act of lovemaking.

Simple? Ha! Loving Matt Kendall would never be simple!

Well, who said Kelly West couldn't pull off a mira-cle? She had the acting skill; she might as well put it to use.

Lowering her lashes in a playfully seductive pose, she reached out and spread her hands on his rib cage. "Now that I've got you where I want you, come closer." And she lay back on the rug, tugging him down with her.

Once again, Kelly's unexpectedly provocative be-havior threw him off balance—in a literal sense this time—and he fell on top of her, an irresistibly good-smelling if somewhat heavy burden that she welcomed with open arms. She could hardly breathe, but she wasn't about to relinquish him. Dear heaven, every hard-muscled inch of him felt like a living dream on top of her! "Mmm . . . perfect. Now things are going ac-cording to my fantasy."

"You mean you *wanted* us to end up on the floor?" he asked faintly.

"Can you think of a better place for . . . this?"

Matt sucked in his breath at the unbelievable feel of her body beneath his, her hands trailing intoxicating fire. With that one move of hers, every muscle in his body had tightened, his mind had snapped to full at-tention and his need had returned with a vengeance. Groaning, he closed his eyes and squeezed her. Con-scious of her thin vulnerability even as he shifted his hips against her, he cautioned himself not to hurt her. It had been so long, so very long, since he'd wanted a woman like he wanted Kelly, and she looked so fragile. And she'd just got over the flu....

An instant later he noticed that her eager hands were gliding down his back and slipping into his shorts. Nor did they stop there. When a waft of cool air whispered over the bare skin of his backside, Matt lifted his head, startled.

Kelly grinned up at him devilishly. "You did want to take those off too, didn't you?"

He bent his head to drop a light kiss on her lips. "Whatever *you* want, honey." Honey was exactly what she tasted like. "It's your fantasy, after all." Rolling to one side, he lay on his back with knees bent, feet planted flat on the floor. "Take me, I'm yours."

"Now that's an offer I can't refuse," Kelly murmured as she finished removing his shorts and athletic supporter, then unlaced his tennis shoes and stripped his feet of socks.

She could hardly keep her eyes off what was undoubtedly the most fascinating part of his anatomy, although she considered it unladylike to stare. He had a rare beauty and grace about him that made other men seem mediocre. Not just physically, she thought. In every way he was special, golden, superior. She loved him.

She *loved* him!

Kelly's gaze just happened to be lingering on the juncture of Matt's thighs when the realization hit her, and she grew perfectly still, her eyes widening at the thought. She really loved him. Not just for his body, although—oh, mercy, what a body he had!

"If you see anything that interests you, feel free to sample the merchandise," he said, his tone amused.

She just continued to stare, her mouth dry.

"On the other hand, if you don't like what you see, I can always get dressed." And he propped himself up on one elbow and reached for his clothes.

Kelly's hand swatted his. "Don't you dare!" Frantically she tried to collect herself. This shocking flash of insight didn't have to change things. Matt was still a dear friend, and he always would be if she had her way. And now more than ever she intended to see to it that tonight worked out for both of them.

He lay watching her, waiting.

Reminding herself that she had control of this fantasy, she took a deep breath and put her hand on him, touching his masculinity with an initial shyness that quickly changed to bold pleasure as she felt his rigid strength. When her fingers curled around the proud shaft, Matt arched his back and absorbed the charges of potent sensation that her hands transmitted to him. He felt on fire, his nerves singing with tension, as if he was wired to a fuse box that was shooting him full of magical, shimmering electricity. His breathing shallow, he threw his head back and spoke through gritted teeth. "Kelly...ahh...you're a witch! Where...oh, Kelly...where on earth did you...ahhh...learn to do this?"

I'm learning right here, right now, she thought distractedly. The hard, warm feel of Matt, the sensually disturbing sight of his well-formed nakedness, the heady male scent of him in the air around her—all were combining to teach her things about passion she had never even imagined before. Wanting to entice him as he was enticing her, she feathered her fingertips along his bare flesh and felt him shudder.

"More," he groaned, reaching for her and pulling her over on top of him. "Please, my sweet Kelly, let me have more of you."

"I want it all, too," she whispered, her voice choked with need. "Matt, I want you to love me."

They came together, their bodies warming each other, their hearts straining for unity. Matt was amazed that they fit together so perfectly, his athletic muscularity complementing her reedlike slimness. She opened to him with an ardor that thrilled him and then closed herself around him with astonishing strength to hold him deep inside so the rapture would last. When he moved, she also moved in a way that drew out the ecstasy, multiplying it, splintering it into a million fragments of light, magnifying it into an experience never to be forgotten. Her teasing, bewitching hands made him aware of his body, aware of his own great capacity to feel, and he gloried in the feeling.

"Kelly, my love—" he kissed her closed eyelids "—can I love you all night?"

She felt his hips rotate against hers and hoped the wild feverish agitation he was provoking wouldn't stop. "As long as you like, Matthew," she panted. "Forever."

In the next instant a symphony of beauty and harmony exploded around them and the moment became forever, and Kelly knew there would never be another like it if she lived to be a hundred. That moment would be trapped in eternity for her to remember: Matt holding her, hot and musky from loving her, trembling with soaring emotions, kissing her throat as he crooned tender words in her ear.

And Matt knew. Lying on the rug, wrapped as tightly around Kelly West as he could get, he knew he loved her. The part of him that he sometimes feared had died all those years ago, now ached in his chest with the sweet, fierce pain of caring too much. Every part of him throbbed with love for her, and he had to close his eyes against the tears. And they were tears of joy.

AFTER A WHILE the pervasive cold seeped up through the rug and penetrated even the snug cocoon Kelly and Matt had spun around themselves. "You awake?" he asked softly from his position beneath her.

"Mm-hmm. Barely." She stirred lazily, relishing every contour and texture of his body, every movement that he made.

"You're really c-crazy about the f-floor, huh?"

There was something funny about the way he was talking. "What do you mean, crazy about the floor?"

"You s-said you had f-fantasized about making love on the f-floor."

She giggled. "I'd have pretended to want to make love in the broom closet if that was where you happened to be." Raising her head, she eyed him critically. "Since when do you stutter, Matthew Kendall?"

"S-since I'm f-freezing my t-tail off." He sat up, shifting her reluctantly to one side. "D-do you m-mind if we get in b-bed now?"

More than willing to comply, she scrambled to her feet and threw back the bedclothes, then brought another quilt from her mother's cedar chest to help warm up the naked shivering hunk who was by now huddled in the middle of her bed. "Poor Matthew," she murmured, rubbing life back into his frigid feet. "I was lying on top so I didn't realize how cold you were getting."

"My feet aren't the only parts that got cold," he informed her.

"Your tush?"

"Like an iceberg!"

"Well, for goodness sake, turn over and let me do something about it!"

Some minutes later, after he had started to thaw, he complained that another of his parts had been in grave danger of frostbite. When he moved her hand to show her what he meant, she felt compelled to point out that as far as she could tell, his entire body was toasty warm. Nevertheless, she assured him that she would leave her hand in place to provide restorative massage should it be needed on an emergency basis.

"Mmmm . . . good idea." He nuzzled her neck, halfway between desire and sleepiness. "You never know when I might come down with an emergency case of frostbite."

Smiling, she gave him a hug back. "Speaking of emergencies, I'm amazed that your beeper has been so quiet all evening."

He stiffened in horror, his face draining of color, and a second later he was out of her arms and groping about madly for his clothes.

Kelly sat up in bed and watched him fearfully. "What's wrong?"

"I left my beeper in the car." His voice was taut and almost inaudible as he yanked the T-shirt over his head and stepped into his shorts. One hand clutching his sweatpants and socks, he headed for the living room, still muttering to himself. "I've never done that before. What was I thinking of?"

Kelly dashed after him with his shoes, afraid that he intended to go outside half dressed, but instead he stopped at the telephone and dialed his answering service. After listening to the operator for a minute, he thanked her, replaced the receiver and sank down on the sofa, looking shaken.

When he silently began drawing on his socks, then the sweatpants, Kelly dropped his shoes and ran to the bedroom for her robe. She returned to find him still seated, tying his shoelaces.

"Matthew?" she said, and he looked up. His brown eyes were puzzled, troubled. "All quiet on the western front?"

"No emergencies."

"Good. Then you can stay."

He hesitated. "I'd like to."

There was something he wasn't saying. "But?"

"I don't know if I should. You . . . I lose track of time around you, Kelly." He summoned a half-hearted grin. "You make me feel young."

"Oh, yeah. Old Dr. Kendall. You're practically in your dotage."

His grin faded. "I've never forgotten my beeper before. I can't believe I left it in the car. If the hospital had tried to reach me—"

"They didn't. You said yourself there was no problem."

"But there might have been."

"Dammit, Matt, a tornado might have suddenly appeared from nowhere and blown us to smithereens, but it didn't!" She threw herself down on the sofa next to him. "You made a mistake. You're human." He looked unconvinced, and she asked impatiently, "How long have you been wearing a beeper?"

"Since my last year in medical school."

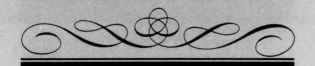

YOUR
PASSPORT
TO
R♥MANCE

HARLEQUIN
VISA
FOR FREE GIFTS

**VALIDATE
YOUR
PASSPORT
TODAY!**

**Send us your Visa and get
4 Free Books, a Free Tote Bag
and your Extra Mystery Gift!**

GO FOR IT ➡

HERE'S YOUR TICKET TO ROMANCE AND A GEM OF AN OFFER!

1. Four FREE Harlequin Romances

Book a free getaway to love with your Harlequin VISA. You'll receive four exciting new romances hot off the presses. All yours, compliments of Harlequin Reader Service. You'll get all the passion, the tender moments and the intrigue of love in far-away places...FREE!

2. A Beautiful Harlequin Tote Bag...Free!

Carry away your favorite romances in your elegant canvas Tote Bag. At a spacious 13 square inches, there'll be lots of room for shopping, sewing and exercise gear, too! With a snap-top and double handles, your Tote Bag is valued at $6.99—but it's yours free with this offer!

3. Free Magazine Subscription

You'll receive our members-only magazine, Harlequin Romance Digest, three times per year. In addition, you'll be up on all the news about your favourite writers, upcoming books and much more with Harlequin's Free monthly newsletter.

4. Free Delivery and 26¢ Off Store Prices

Join Harlequin Reader Service today and discover the convenience of Free home delivery. You'll preview four exciting new books each month—and pay only $1.99 per book. That's 26¢ less than the store price. It all adds up to one gem of an offer!

YOU'LL GET A FREE MYSTERY GIFT TOO!

USE YOUR HARLEQUIN VISA TO VALIDATE YOUR PASSPORT TO ROMANCE—APPLY YOUR VISA TO THE POST-PAID CARD ATTACHED AND MAIL IT TODAY!

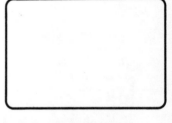

"And you've forgotten it *once* in all that time? What are you trying for, sainthood?"

"That's me," he said wryly. "Saint Matthew."

"Listen, you may be joking, but I'm not. You've got everybody in Parker County convinced. In four days I've received half a dozen invitations to join your fan club."

His lips twitched. "And you said no?"

"Darn right!" She picked up his hand and brought it to her mouth so she could kiss his palm. "I intend to start my own club. Just you and me."

"A mutual admiration society, I hope."

"Uh-uh. You don't need someone else to worship you." Turning his hand over, she ran the tip of her tongue along the back of each finger until she felt him shiver.

"What do I need?" he asked hoarsely.

"You need someone to make you relax—to help you stop being such a paragon of virtue every single minute of every single day."

"Relax, hmm?" He shut his eyes and leaned his head back against the cushion. "Is this what you call relaxing me?"

"At least it's a start. Give me a few more hours and we'll get *all* of you relaxed." She patted the most noticeably unrelaxed portion of his body, and he almost choked.

"Ahhh . . . !" He sat up abruptly. "Really, Kelly, I should go."

"But you don't want to," she argued reasonably.

"Oh, no. I don't want to." Sighing, he stood up and moved away from her.

"If it would make you feel any better, we could drive over and check on your grandmother, then come back here."

"My grandmother—" He swung to face her again, his expression distracted. "You want to hear something funny? My answering service took a message from Jenny. She and Bill stopped by after the game to see Grandma, and she went home with them to spend the night."

Kelly's heart did a joyous somersault. *Thank you, Jenny!* "I'm sure they'll all have a good visit."

Matt put his fists on his hips and stared at Kelly as if she'd lost her mind. "Grandma never goes out in weather like this."

"So . . . for once Jenny talked her into it."

"Just like that?" He shook his head. "I wouldn't be surprised if she promised Grandma you and I will get married."

Kelly had heard of worse ideas, but maybe Matt hadn't. He was looking a little harassed. Better bypass that topic.

"Look, Matt, it's no big deal," she said as breezily as she could. "You already said you want to stay so there's no reason why you shouldn't. Grandma Bowen will be safe and sound at Jenny's, and you left my number with your service. They can call you here if they need to."

He kept waiting for her to say she wanted him to stay, but she didn't. He would have forced the issue if he hadn't feared she didn't really care one way or the other. He wanted her to care as much as he did, which he supposed wasn't very likely.

At least she hadn't mentioned Luke John in three hours.

"Do you suppose," she was saying, "we could get rid of the noble Dr. Kendall for a while so you and I can enjoy what's left of the night?"

He pretended to frown at her. "Don't you like Dr. Kendall?"

"Sure I like him. If you want to know the truth, I *love* him. But I don't particularly want to fool around with a saint. Especially one who never forgets to wear his beeper to bed."

Matt tried to hold the scowl, but despite himself a grin escaped. She loved him! Maybe not the same way he loved her, but it was a start.

Strolling over to the couch, he stood looking down at the slivers of light caught in her copper-colored hair. Her green witch's eyes watched him with forthright interest, and he knew she was worth any risk. All right, dammit, he would force the issue.

His hand stretched out to her, his fingers furrowing into the thick glossy waves until they brushed her scalp. He saw smoky fires flare up in her eyes, and he suspected his own eyes were starting to smolder. "Are you saying you want to fool around with *me*?"

She stood and put her hands on his lean waist, pleased to note that he kept his fingers tangled in her hair. "That all depends. Just which Matthew Kendall are you—the saint or the sinner?"

He slid his free hand inside the gaping neckline of her robe and traced a fingertip along her collarbone, then down in a tantalizing detour around her nipple. "Try me," he suggested in a throaty whisper. "I'm a match for Lucia St. Claire any day."

"Is that a fact?" Kelly's eyes glittered with excitement as she wound her arms around him. "We'll just have to see about that."

They lost no time in returning to bed so they could put Matt's claim to the test. Two hours later Kelly lay sprawled half on, half off his body, totally naked, the covers strewn about in disarray. "Whew! You're better than central heating, Matthew. I can vouch for that!"

"It did get a little steamy there for a while, didn't it?"

"For a while? You're inexhaustible!"

"I come of hardy Romanian stock, ladychik. My blood iss red. I strong. I tink you find I not tiring easi-leek."

His tone was grave, his accent ridiculous, but none-theless recognizable. Kelly sat bolt upright. "Where on earth did you hear that?"

"On *California Dreaming*, ladychik."

"I know where you heard it. That was Petru Lipatti talking, and his storyline was on a year ago. What I mean is, what were you doing watching *California Dreaming* in the first place?"

He doubled up a pillow and stuffed it beneath his head, grinning at her discomposure. "I was in bed with a cold for a week last January. Since Grandma watched your show, I did, too."

"Every day?" He nodded. "Weren't you bored?"

"Bored? Fat chance! It took me all of ten minutes to get good and hooked. I almost hated to go back to work when I got well. Ever since then, if I make my hospital rounds when *California Dreaming* is on the air, I find myself sneaking a peek at the nearest television."

Kelly plopped back beside him, trying to imagine the dedicated Dr. Kendall sitting glued to a TV set while his patients languished. She swiveled her head and stud-ied him curiously. "What did you find so fascinating?"

"The same thing that fascinated everybody else. Lucia. It was an education watching her seduce . . . what's his name? Petra?"

"Petru Lipatti. The Romanian immigrant. He's no longer on the show."

"I know that. Honey, I watched her stab him in the heart with a wooden stake. That ladychik had guts. No scruples but plenty of guts."

"She thought he was a vampire." When Matt hooted, she poked him in the ribs. "She really did, Matthew! You probably don't know the entire story behind it, but Lucia had a deep irrational fear of vampires that was rooted in her childhood."

"The operative word here being irrational."

"Well, she *did* get off on a plea of temporary insanity." Kelly snapped her fingers. "Oh, shoot. You didn't happen to see my trial, did you?"

"Lucia's trial? No, I regret that I didn't have the pleasure."

"Too bad. Those were some of the best dramatic moments of my career."

Matt figured Kelly's career hadn't lacked for dramatic moments. For the hundredth time he wondered how she would ever adjust to living in Weatherford again, but he deliberately shoved the doubts to the back of his mind, out of sight. Tonight was too special to waste on such futile speculation. Tonight Kelly had brought him back to life, and he wanted to enjoy every minute with her.

Rolling onto his side, he scooped her close and began kissing her with an intensity that was both unexpected and supremely pleasurable. He eased one knee between her legs and let his muscular, hair-roughened thigh do the work of arousing her, nudging slowly, gently, persistently closer to his goal.

"Matthew, what are you doing to me?" she gasped after a moment.

"Sshh!" He pulled the sheet up over their heads, shutting out the lamplight. "I'm just trying to make a little drama for us."

Kelly felt herself melting against the rising heat. "Oh, babe, I'll help!"

8

SINCE THE LINE at the drive-through window consisted of more than three cars, Kelly opted to park and place her order inside the fast-food establishment. There were half a dozen customers already at the counter, but the lively atmosphere more than compensated for her wait. The gray day outside didn't fit her mood at all.

The plain truth was that she felt too good to sit in the car. She beamed indiscriminately at those ahead of her, certain they must all guess that last night had been the most spectacular night of her life. Thanks entirely to Matt Kendall.

Oh, yes, she thought with a shiver, a thousand thanks to Matthew Kendall!

She pirouetted out of sheer nervous energy and bumped into the rotund gentleman who had entered behind her. "Excuse me!" She bestowed a huge smile on him, glad to have a reason to speak. "I should be more careful."

"No harm done," the man assured her with a twinkle in his eye. "Nice to see you, Miss West. I'm glad you've recovered from your flu."

"Thank you." She gave him a closer look. He seemed familiar, but she couldn't quite place him.

He understood her dilemma and extended a plump white hand. "Phillip Farnsworth," he said amiably.

"Of course, Mr. Farnsworth." She clasped his hand. "It *is* good to see you." He was president of the bank that had handled her parents' financial affairs all of Kelly's life. "Goodness, it's been a few years, hasn't it?"

"And more than a few pounds, eh?" He patted his portly stomach and chuckled. His gray hair had thinned, too, but the gallant kindness that Kelly remembered still seemed a vital part of his nature.

As soon as she ordered her food and turned to speak to him again, the banker grew earnest. "I wonder if you might let me buy you lunch one day soon. There's something I need to discuss with you."

Kelly's brow knit at his tone. "Is there a problem with my mother's estate?"

He looked surprised. "No, nothing like that. The fact is, I'm chairman of the board of directors of the Weatherford Performing Arts Association, Miss West. I hadn't intended to get into that here, but I don't want you worrying that there's anything wrong. As a matter of fact, I'm aware of several needs the community has in the field of dramatic arts, and some of us on the board would like to interest you in meeting those needs."

Her mouth dropped open, and several seconds passed before she remembered to close it.

"I'm talking about employment, not volunteer work," Mr. Farnsworth hastened to add, reading her astonishment as reluctance. "I understand you have a degree in drama from Baylor University, as well as some postgraduate work in London?"

"I studied at the Royal Academy of Dramatic Arts for a year," she affirmed with a nod.

"Excellent background." Glancing around, he leaned closer to Kelly. "What would you think of a teaching post at the college?"

"The . . . college? Weatherford College?"

"That's right. They could use a theater director with your hands-on experience."

Don't babble, Kelly, she commanded herself, and took a long slow breath. "It sounds intriguing."

"Good. I'll call you about lunch."

"Do that." She gave him another of her famous smiles, collected her order from the cashier and floated out to the BMW on a cloud. Imagine Kelly West a college professor!

By the time she reached Annie Bowen's neat brick bungalow, Kelly had put the encounter in perspective. However promising, it wasn't a firm job offer. Better not mention it to Matt until she discussed it further with Mr. Farnsworth.

"Hello, Grandma Bowen," she greeted the thin, stooped lady who opened the door to her knock. "Do you know who I am?"

"No-o-o, I don't think so." Her voice was silvery. So was her short, fine hair. She peered at Kelly through eyes clouded by age.

"I'm Charlotte West's daughter, Kelly."

"Oh, my . . . Kelly?" Laughing with pleasure, Mrs. Bowen motioned her inside and spread her arms wide. Kelly gave her a one-sided but enthusiastic hug, balancing the big bag of take-out food in her other hand.

When she finally released Kelly, the old lady had tears in her eyes. "I don't know why I didn't recognize you, honey. You look so much like your mama. Bless my soul, I miss Charlotte!"

"Me, too." Determined to cheer up the lady who had been such a dear friend to her mother, Kelly shook the bag of chicken. "Look, Grandma Bowen. I brought lunch for us." She hadn't been certain that Jenny would have dropped her grandmother off at home by noon, but she had ordered plenty of food just in case.

"Wonderful! I love fried chicken. When you came, I was just checking to see what I could fix for lunch."

"Lead the way to the kitchen, and I'll get this ready," Kelly suggested.

She urged Annie to sit down at the table and let Kelly do all the work, and after an initial protest Matt's grandmother agreed. As Kelly hunted through the cabinets, Mrs. Bowen asked about her trip from California.

"It could have been worse," Kelly conceded, putting out two plates. "I suppose I could have collapsed *before* I reached Weatherford." She would have been in a fine mess then!

"You collapsed?" Grandma clicked her tongue. "Well, forevermore! Were you sick?"

Kelly's hand paused at the task of folding a pair of linen napkins. It had been just four days since Mrs. Bowen had sent a pot of chicken soup to the invalid. Had she forgotten? "Yes, I had the flu. Matt took care of me."

"Well, he must have done a good job. You look fine now, honey. You're a mighty pretty girl." Absently Kelly smiled her thanks. "What was it you did out there in California? Weren't you in the movies?"

A tight worried ache began in Kelly's chest at the question. Despite Rita's warning, she had expected Grandma Bowen's mind to be as sharp as it was six years ago. The ache spread when she opened the silverware drawer and found a plastic freezer bag containing sliced ham that was soggy and partially thawed. She chewed her lip. "I was on television." She lifted the bag and carried it, dripping, to the sink. "Grandma, did you put this in the drawer?" she asked with assumed nonchalance.

Mrs. Bowen seemed puzzled. "I don't know how it got there. I was planning to eat that ham for lunch before you came." She frowned. "I sometimes find things in the strangest places around here."

Before Kelly could think of a response, the telephone rang. From listening to one end of the conversation, she deduced that it was Rita Kendall calling with an offer to bring lunch for her mother, but Mrs. Bowen assured her she was going to eat in style—with Matt's wife!

Kelly's heart jumped into her throat.

"Oh, you know who I mean, Rita," Annie hurried on with flustered impatience. "Kelly. Charlotte's girl. She brought over some fried chicken for our lunch. Yes, wasn't that sweet of her? We're having a nice visit. I will, dear. All right. Goodbye."

"I don't know why I called you Matt's wife," Mrs. Bowen mumbled half to herself as she went back to her seat. "Unless it's because I always wished you two kids would get married."

Clearing her throat, Kelly put the platter of chicken and the basket of rolls in the middle of the table. "Did you really?"

There was nothing foggy about the expression in Grandma's eyes now. "Ever since you were five years old."

"Why?"

"Because you're just what Matt needs."

Kelly poked a big spoon into the potato salad and another into the coleslaw and then took the chair opposite Annie. "What do you mean? Matt seems pretty self-sufficient to me. Besides, we don't have all that much in common."

"Phooey." Grandma waved aside Kelly's cautious denial. "You and Luke John—there have been plenty who predicted you two would get married, both of you being celebrities and all. But I knew better. Luke John wouldn't want to compete with a wife." She chuckled fondly. "That boy wants all the attention himself. Now Matt." Her expression changed subtly to reveal the wealth of tender love she had for the grandson who made his home with her. "Matt's strong and independent, all right, but his heart gets him hurt every time. People drain him. They take everything he's got to offer, and he keeps on doling it out until he's flat empty. He needs someone to give him a reason to hold back a little. He needs someone to come home to, other than an old woman like me." Kelly looked at her in silence, her eyes blurring. "What he needs is a spunky little spitfire like you, Kelly." Annie laughed again, remembering. "You could whip a dozen wildcats, even when you were knee-high to a tadpole. You wouldn't let anyone take advantage of Matt's kind heart, would you?"

"No," she muttered, hastily wiping at her unspitfirelike tears. If she could, she'd guard him fiercely from his own goodness. She'd insist that he get plenty of sleep and eat regular meals and take on no more cases that were certain to break his heart. She would—

The abrupt opening and closing of the kitchen door interrupted Kelly's mental declaration of her intentions. She looked up, and a golden glow suffused her at the sight of the object of those intentions. Matt stood there, as much a hunk in tweed sport coat and slacks as he had been last night in absolutely nothing.

"Hello!" He sounded out of breath, and his surprised brown eyes swept from Kelly to his grandmother and back again.

She felt a sudden flash of terror that she had become an overnight embarrassment to him—that he regretted making love to her and didn't want to see her again.

A second later he smiled, and warmth and pleasure lit the velvet darkness of his eyes.

"My contribution to your lunch," he informed Annie with a grin, holding up a brown paper bag from the deli. He opened the refrigerator and stuck it inside. "Looks like you didn't need my tuna salad after all."

"Bless your heart, you don't have to come home and check on me," Mrs. Bowen said. "Sit down and eat, darlin'. I'll get you a plate."

"No, Gran, thanks. I can't stay." He trailed a hand affectionately across Annie's back as he passed her chair and then stopped behind Kelly. Gripping her shoulders with long, cool fingers, he bent close and brushed his mouth across her cheek to her ear. "Can't you even tell me good morning?" he murmured.

She breathed in his scent and closed her eyes for a moment, forgetting his grandmother, who sat in satisfied silence, watching the little scene. "Good morning, Matthew."

He gave her a squeeze before he straightened. "That's better. It hurts my feelings when you ignore me."

Ignore him! Was it possible to ignore a man so beautiful inside and out that he inspired unforgettable fantasies, so dynamically vital that he could warm up a room just by coming into it? Kelly pondered the question as he reached past her for a drumstick and took a bite.

"I wish I could stay a while, but . . ." His voice trailed off, and he shrugged an apology, his mind already winging ahead to the afternoon's hectic schedule. When would he find the time to run by the hospital and check on Mary Wilson? He leaned a hip against the counter and munched on the chicken leg thoughtfully.

"You'd be bored stiff," Kelly assured him, and he looked at her dubiously. Bored with Kelly around? Not likely. "I'm going to prevail upon your grandmother to teach me to quilt, if she has the patience."

Annie's eyes brightened, and Matt felt his throat constrict. The old lady usually considered herself unneeded despite all the family's efforts to convince her otherwise. "Grandma, can I borrow Kelly for a minute? I want her to walk me to my car."

"It's cold out there, Matt," Annie said. "She's been sick, you know. Don't let her get a chill."

"I wouldn't dream of it." He caught Kelly's hand and tugged her to her feet. Taking off his jacket, he draped it around her as they went outside. One strong arm encircled her waist as they crossed the yard to his Blazer. "You're a nice person, Kelly West," he said gruffly.

"You're just saying that because you want my body."

"No, I'm saying it because it's true."

"Then you *don't* want my body?"

"I want your body so bad I can taste it, and that's beside the point. You're still nice."

"So are you, doctor. So now we're even."

"How's that?"

"I want your body, too." They had reached his car and stopped, and she turned to face him and grasp his shirt front. Leaning forward until their hips met, she ran her tongue across his lower lip in an unbearably sensual kiss, all the more arousing because it was so light and feathery.

Matt's breath caught, and he grabbed her to him for a fierce hug, then held her off a little. "Please, Miss West! Not here. What will the neighbors think?"

"That I'm protecting you from frostbite?"

"Uh-uh. They don't even know I'm susceptible to frostbite. They'll think *one* of us has hyperactive hormones."

"Only one of us? I thought our hormones were in perfect harmony."

He chuckled wickedly. "They are kind of . . . mmm . . . friendly, aren't they?"

"Congenial, compatible, cozy—that's us. Me and my hormones only have one complaint. You were gone when we woke up this morning!"

"Believe me, I hated to climb out of your warm bed, honey, but my days start early."

Was her warm bed the only thing he hated to leave? "Next time, wake me," she said. "I'm used to being at the studio by six."

Would there be a next time? He hoped so with all his heart. "Listen, Kelly, if you're not busy tonight, how about running over to Fort Worth with me?" He tossed it out casually, as if he hadn't been plotting this half the morning. "We can eat Mexican at Joe T. Garcia's."

"I love Mexican food, and I'm not busy."

"Good. I'll pick you up at seven, hmm?" He glanced at his watch and released her with a grimace. "If I finish by then." He kissed her once more, then took his coat when she held it out to him. "Kelly, thank you for being so good with Grandma."

He was gone before she could answer, leaving her to wonder whether he had invited her to dinner in appreciation for her friendship with his grandmother, or because he, like Kelly, had fallen much too far to stop himself.

MATT HUNG UP THE PAY TELEPHONE in the lobby, turned a set of broad and unfriendly shoulders toward the young lady at the concession stand who was staring at him and strode back into the theater. He paused just beyond the double doors so his eyes could adjust once more to the darkness. Annoyed to find himself sweating lightly, he ran a hand across his upper lip. He *hated* going to the movies. If his date were anyone but Kelly, he wouldn't be there now.

After leaving the restaurant, she had seen the marquee and had started bullying him to take her to one of Luke John's old films playing there. Thanks to some fast double-talk, he had managed to finesse her into one of the other shows, but he could tell she was disappointed. She must have really wanted to see Luke John.

He looked down the aisle and picked her out of the crowd. There was something compelling about her even in the dimness, and with the heart-pounding hunger that had plagued him nearly a week now, he suddenly had to get back to her, to touch her and make sure she didn't go away.

When he sat down beside her, she caught his hand and laced their fingers together. "What took you so long?" she whispered. "Is everything okay?"

"Fine. I just wanted to check in and make sure." He'd been afraid Mary might have problems, although her blood pressure seemed to be under control these days.

She patted his knee. "Watch the movie, then. You've missed the best part so far."

Sliding down obediently low in the plush seat, he stuck out one long leg in the aisle and tried to make the other fit into the available space. He tucked an arm around Kelly and pulled her against him and, as if by magic, the aftereffects of his eighteen-hour day began to fade. Rigid neck muscles and taut nerves relaxed, and he stopped gritting his teeth. Slowly he breathed in, then exhaled in a soft sigh.

Kelly was glad she had seen this movie before, because she suddenly found it impossible to concentrate on Sly Stallone. There were too many distractions. Matt's clean fragrance, for instance—by now a familiar and sensually disturbing scent. His body heat and the supple steel of his arm and thigh. The gentle rhythm of his breathing...the weight of his head nodding sideways against hers....

What was he doing? "Matt?" she whispered, and nudged him with her elbow. When she got no response, she peeked at him out of the corner of her eye and had to smile. He'd fallen asleep, right smack dab in the middle of what Kelly suspected was the first movie he'd gone to in years. All those middle-of-the-night emergencies and early mornings had caught up with him at last. Or maybe it was just last night in particular.

She let him sleep, propping him up long past the point that her entire body went numb from lack of movement. When the credits finished rolling up the screen and the lights came on, he still slept. Even the noise of the crowd vacating the theater didn't wake him. Kelly attributed all the stares the two of them received to the fact that her date was noticeably unconscious.

Although, she admitted, a few of the moviegoers might have recognized her as Lucia St. Claire.

Finally Kelly and Matt were the only ones left, and she had no choice but to rouse him. "Okay, Matthew," she said, "time to go home."

"Mmmhmm," he agreed, scrunching down farther, his nose buried against her neck.

"Let's go." She jiggled her shoulder against him, causing his head to wobble up and down, but he snoozed on obliviously. "Come on, doctor, cooperate!" Exasperated, she used both hands to push him upright in the seat. Jumping to her feet, she stood over him, hands on his shoulders, and shook him.

"Mmph!" he protested, and popped open dark, bemused eyes. He blinked sleepily at Kelly, then glanced around, yawning. "Where is everyone?"

"If they're smart, they've gone home to bed, which is where you should have been hours ago, Matt. I'm sorry I talked you into a movie."

"'Sokay." He yawned again and stood up, enveloping her in a tight hug. "I wasn't ready to go home yet." He bent his head to rub his cheek against the thick softness of her hair. "Was it a good show?"

"I didn't watch the show. I watched you. Now *that* was good!"

Shaking his head wryly, he turned and started up the aisle. He figured it had been a long time since she'd gone out with such a live wire. What a jerk, he chided himself, to ask Kelly West for a date and then fall asleep on her!

When they reached the lobby, he let his gaze wander admiringly down Kelly's slender length in her green silk blouse and black slacks, then glanced over at the cluster of theater patrons who waited by the doors. Apparently the lingerers were reluctant to go out into the cold night. "I have a feeling we shouldn't have left your coat in the car, Kelly."

She opened her mouth to answer him, but never got a chance. A high, excited squeal shrilled through the lobby, and the girl who had worked the concession stand darted over to them from the crowd.

"I knew it! It *is* him!" Stopping right in front of Matt, she beckoned over her shoulder. "It's Luke John Kendall!"

A second later Matt was surrounded by a passel of wild-eyed females waving pens and scraps of paper. Amused, Kelly stood back and watched. She'd seen the same thing happen in Hollywood nearly every time she went anywhere with Luke John. Relishing such displays of hero worship, the real Luke could sign autographs all night long.

Matt looked as if he wanted to drop through the floor. He kept opening his mouth—Kelly had a pretty good idea what he was trying to say—but the noise level had risen so high, no one could hear him.

He turned his blond head and looked at Kelly in mute appeal. Seeing the barely veiled panic in his eyes, she had a hard time keeping a straight face. She shrugged and lifted her open palms to him in a gesture that said she was helpless to rescue him.

Perplexed, Matt raked his fingers through his hair. The resulting tousled look and the traces of fatigue still evident around his eyes gave Kelly's heart a distinct jolt, and she could just imagine how it was affecting all his impressionable "fans." They seemed on the verge of swooning.

"Sign my checkbook, Luke John!" a dressed-for-success young businesswoman begged him.

"I'm not Luke John Kendall." Matt spoke clearly into the sudden lull. "You're mistaking me for someone else."

The crowd hooted at that idea. "You can't fool us, Luke John. We'd know you anywhere!"

"Yeah, and besides, you're with *her*." And they pointed at Kelly.

"I've got pictures of you all over my walls, Luke John," a teenager shouted.

"He's even finer in person than his pictures."

Nodding her agreement, Kelly turned to see who had uttered the compliment. A collegiate preppy wearing L.L. Bean and looking totally awestruck held out a loose-leaf notebook to her. "Miss West, would you mind very much signing this? *California Dreaming* just isn't the same these days without you."

Kelly autographed the notebook with a smile before swinging her gaze back to Matt.

"I am *not* Luke John Kendall!" He had mastered the panic. Now he merely sounded frustrated. Everyone ignored his denial.

"My mother'll kill me if I don't bring home your autograph!" someone wailed, thrusting a torn envelope under his nose.

Rolling his eyes, Matt clamped shut his mouth and frowned at Kelly as if this were all her fault. Without another word, he snatched the envelope and scribbled something across it, then took the next paper and then the next until the crowd started to thin out. Kelly leaned against the nearby wall and chuckled to herself, admiring the way he was handling the experience. While she was graciously accommodating another request for Lucia's signature, he appeared at her side, took the pen from her hand unceremoniously and returned it to its owner.

"Let's go."

His voice was low and firm. She could imagine him giving orders at the hospital in that exact tone. She couldn't imagine anyone disobeying.

"Yessir!"

They crossed the parking lot in record time, and Matt all but picked her up and tossed her into the Blazer. When he got behind the wheel, he looked in the rear-view mirror as if he expected to be pursued all the way home.

She put her hand on his leg and felt the muscles flex as he revved up the engine. "Calm down, Matthew. You gave them what they want, so you're safe. They'll leave you alone."

Reaching out to flip on the heater, he asked tautly, "What do you mean, I gave them what they want?"

"They wanted Luke John's autograph, and you gave it to them."

He turned to glare at her. "You think I signed Luke's name?"

"Well . . . didn't you?"

He drew a ragged, very angry breath. "My name is Matthew Mark Kendall. That's the name I signed back there because, damn it all, I won't pretend to be something I'm not. If you want to strut around on the arm of the hotshot Luke Kendall, you shouldn't be here now, with me."

He lifted his foot from the brake, and they shot off down the street while Kelly tried to figure out what had happened. Where in heaven's name did he get the idea she would rather be with Luke John? The force of his outburst stunned her, but it didn't hamper her ability to reason. She sensed that Matt had attacked her simply because she was handy.

She also knew the moment that he made the same realization. Halfway to Weatherford, she heard him sigh and felt the Blazer slow down as he eased up on the accelerator.

"I'm sorry," he muttered.

"You should be."

"I just want to be sure you understand, Kelly. Any similarity between my brother and me is purely superficial."

"You think I don't know that?" she snapped. "I've known you and Luke John all my life. Old jokes notwithstanding, I'm quite capable of telling you two apart. But I'd like to know what's the big deal about a few of his fans making a perfectly natural mistake?"

"No big deal. I overreacted."

"Yeah, I noticed."

He sighed again. "You aren't going to make this easy, are you?"

She shrugged in an elaborate show of nonchalance. "Why should I? I'm not the one who behaved like an idiot."

"I said I'm sorry." He sent her a wounded look calculated to melt the hardest heart. "You could have prevented the whole thing in the first place, you know. Why didn't you tell those people they had the wrong Kendall?"

"You think they'd have believed *me*?"

"I guess not. Okay, I accept full responsibility for any idiot behavior that took place between us tonight. Do you forgive me?"

He glanced over at her with a hopeful grin, and Kelly's heart assumed the consistency of hot butter. "That depends," she said gruffly, fighting the effects of that crooked grin.

"On what?"

"On you. Tell me something, Matt. What happened between you and Luke?"

His smile vanishing, he faced the windshield. "Ahhh . . . nothing. Not a thing."

Which translated as "don't push." Kelly heeded the unspoken warning, and they drove the rest of the way in silence, not exactly companionable, but not hostile, either.

When Matt walked her to her front door, he stood with his hands on her shoulders, his chin resting on top of her head. She smelled sweet and clean, and his heart ached with all he couldn't say to her. "I guess I'm not invited in tonight, hmm?"

He would always be welcome in her home—in her bed, too, for that matter—but Kelly thought she'd better not tell him that.

He grunted. "Maybe it's just as well. I think my batteries need recharging."

"You work too hard."

"Yeah. Kelly—" he straightened and curved a hand along her cheek, tipping her face up to his "—I want to see you again soon."

"I'm going back to see your grandmother tomorrow. She says I'm a fast learner."

"I'm sure you are. I'll probably come by at noon." It wasn't exactly what he had in mind, but he guessed it would have to do.

She studied his expression a minute. "Matt? Would you take me to the football game Friday night?"

He hesitated. "It's in Lubbock."

"No kidding, Sherlock. Tell you what. If your batteries are still low, I'll drive and you can sleep on the way."

"I don't know, Kelly. I'll have to see how things stand with my patients. And that's not fair to you—to keep you waiting for an answer." He ran a hand through his hair. "Oh, hell! I want to take you. I just don't know if I can."

"The world isn't going to stop spinning if you go to a football game, doctor. You're not the center of the universe."

"Ouch." He winced. "You're great for my ego."

"Sorry. If it makes you feel any better, I don't mind waiting for your answer. If I can't go with you, I don't want to go at all." And she touched her lips to his in a warmly tantalizing kiss that unleashed wild fire in his loins.

"Lady," he growled when she finally pulled back, "you'd better get inside while you still can. My batteries may be low, but they're not dead."

Laughing softly, she whispered good-night and slipped away.

9

THE KNOCK AT THE FRONT DOOR came at the worst possible time. The telephone had been ringing for what seemed like an eternity to Kelly, who crouched on hands and knees in the living room amid a vivid sea of color, afraid to move.

Slowly she got to her feet, being careful not to disturb the pattern of bright diamond-shaped scraps of cloth that she had laid out in a huge star design on the rug. Treading on tiptoes, she made her way across the fragile floor covering and snatched up the phone.

"Hello!" Her tone reflected impatience at the interruption.

There was a pause, then a hesitant, "Kelly?"

"Yes?" Kelly couldn't concentrate on identifying the voice while the pounding continued in the background. "Hold on a minute. I have to get the door."

Just as she put down the receiver, Jenny breezed into the room. "Hey, whatsa matter, kid? Don't you answer your door anymore?"

"Stop!" Kelly shouted. "Don't come another step!"

Jenny froze in alarm. "What did I do?"

"You almost ruined my quilt! Don't you dare budge from that spot until I tell you." She picked up the phone again. "This is Kelly West. Can I help you?"

"No, but from the sound of it, I can help *you*. Come on back to Hollywood, Kelly."

She slumped against the arm of the sofa. "Oh. Hi, Doug."

"You hear the voice of sanity in a world of loony tunes and all you can say is 'oh, hi, Doug'?"

She laughed dutifully. "How're things going?"

"We miss you, babe. It's just not the same on the set anymore. The cast and crew all want you to come back. Fans, too. Bernard's got about a million letters."

"Naw. They'll forget in no time."

"Fame is fleeting, that's for sure. That's why you need to cash in on this popularity windfall and come back before everyone forgets Lucia St. Claire."

"I was kind of hoping that even after they forget Lucia they'll remember me."

"Don't count on it, doll."

That was one thing about Doug—he didn't mince words.

Glancing idly at Jenny, Kelly saw her shrug out of her coat and draw back her arm to toss it clear across the room onto a chair. The thought of what the resulting down draft would do to her quilt design activated Kelly's vocal cords. "No!" she shrieked, and Jenny clasped the coat to her in real terror. "Sorry, Doug," Kelly spoke into the receiver, "but I've got to go. One of my loony-tune friends is trying to escape from her cage."

She hung up and pivoted. "Well? What do you think?"

"Way to go." Jenny nodded vigorously. "That Doug Barron is all wrong for you. I'm glad to hear you got rid of him."

"No, I mean, what do you think of my quilt?" She motioned at the floor with a broad, sweeping wave of one hand.

"Oh, that." Jenny considered it gravely. "It's gorgeous, but it'll probably be a little tricky sleeping under it. One sneeze and it'll fly apart in every direction."

Kelly scowled as she took her friend's coat and draped it over a footstool near the fire. "Cute, Jenny. You know perfectly well that I intend to piece it together first."

Jenny giggled and then studied the variegated display for another minute. "Honestly, I like the Lone Star design, and these are the most outstanding colors I've ever seen. The blue background is really stunning. Where'd you ever get all this material? It looks like silks and satins..." She knelt and touched a piece tentatively. "Velvet! Lord, Kelly, these were all your beautiful party dresses, weren't they?"

"That's right." Kelly was enormously pleased with herself for having discovered such a practical use for the dresses. She also felt more than a little proud that she had cut out what must have been at least a million diamonds since she had got up that morning. "I'd like to give this to your mother for Christmas."

Jenny made a skeptical face. "Do you know when Christmas is?"

"A week from Monday."

"Uh-huh. And do you have any idea how long it's going to take you to piece this together? Not to mention quilt it?"

"Hey, Jenny, I said I'd like to give it to Rita for Christmas. I didn't say *which* Christmas. I'm not entirely out of touch with reality, you know."

"That's a relief." She stood up. "Now what's this news flash going around about you persuading my brother to go to the game tonight?"

"I did? We're going?" Kelly's exhaustion vanished, and she beamed at Jenny. "I haven't heard from Matt yet."

"Word is, he's trying to juggle things around so you can both go. Last night when he stopped by the drugstore, he told Bill he had asked Dr. McKettrick to cover for him."

Excitement always stimulated Kelly's appetite. Suddenly ravenous, she steered Jenny recklessly around the outer edges of the quilt scraps and into the kitchen, where she sat her down for lunch. Plopping the makings of sandwiches down on the table between them, she began plastering mustard, ham and Swiss cheese on slices of rye bread. "When are you guys leaving?"

"Bill's taking off at noon, and Mom didn't even open her shop today. She's persuaded Dad to skip the Friday afternoon auction at the Fort Worth stockyards so we can all drive up together after lunch. I'd give anything if you and Matt could go with us."

It was still a little hard for Kelly to believe they were going at all. "That would have been fun, but I'm not going to complain." She'd rather have Matt all to herself anyway. "What about Grandma Bowen?"

"Miss Harcomber from church is going to spend the night with her, although Grandma usually makes it just fine by herself when Matt stays out late." Jenny's brown eyes danced. "Like the other night. Grandma told me Matt kept you out *sinfully* late." She chuckled with obvious relish.

"Is that funny?"

"I just wish I could have seen Matt's expression the next morning when she advised him that a sweet girl like you had a reputation to protect. She told him he'd better marry you before he sullied yours. I swear, those were her exact words. I'm quoting Grandma."

No wonder Matt had acted so odd yesterday when he'd joined them for lunch! Kelly groaned. "Well, that cinches it! Matt won't take me to the game. I'll be lucky if he ever speaks to me again."

"Are you kidding? I'm telling you, he wants to go."

"Uh-uh!" Shaking her head, Kelly thrust aside her sandwich. "You're mistaken. The way he feels about Meredith, he won't allow anyone to suggest that he replace her. Not even if it's done in a joking manner, and Grandma Bowen wasn't joking, was she?"

"No, but I'm telling you I'm not wrong. Matt's changed since you came back. I swear, Kelly, he's got a kind of . . . I know this sounds weird, but he's got this glow about him that's been missing for a long time. He's acting young again." She laughed. "Shoot, Kelly, having you around makes me feel young. Is it so strange that it works for him, too?"

"I think you're reading too much into this one date. A date that, I might add, hasn't even been positively confirmed."

When four hours later Kelly still hadn't heard from Matt, she began to get worried. Calling his office, she learned that it had closed at noon and all calls were being handled by Dr. McKettrick.

Dressed for the game, thinking that Matt must be on last-minute rounds, Kelly drove to the lovely knoll where the three-storied Campbell Memorial Hospital overlooked the south part of town. When she spotted his Blazer in the doctors' parking lot, she drove on to find a parking space herself.

As she entered the attractive brown brick building, Kelly glanced at the closed doors of the chapel on her right, then peered ahead down the long hall. Matt could be anywhere. With a sigh, she turned to the information desk and found it unoccupied.

"May I help you?"

A small lady in a neat blue pinafore stepped out of the gift shop, and Kelly turned, smiling gratefully. "Oh, I hope so. I'm trying to find Dr. Kendall. I saw his car outside—"

"Yes, Dr. Kendall's been here all afternoon." The volunteer, whose name tag said she was Oleta Rickles, had an exceptionally sweet face, which suddenly took on a worried expression. "He's delivering a baby just now, or he was the last time I heard."

The thought made Kelly's smile broaden—the very idea that Matt was perhaps right this minute bringing a new life into the world, a tiny, squirming, hungry little person who would be very much loved and welcomed by some family. He had a terrific job, she thought enviously.

Checking her wristwatch, she guessed that even allowing another hour for him to finish whatever a doctor did after delivering a baby, they might still get to see most of the game.

"About how long do deliveries take, on the average?" she asked.

Mrs. Rickles smiled. "On the average? Not as long as Dr. Matt's been in there today. But this one isn't an average delivery, sugar. He's taking the baby by cesarean."

That accounted for her worried look, Kelly thought. "Oh, darn. I'll bet it's Mary Wilson's baby."

The older woman nodded. "Are you a friend of the Wilsons, dear?"

"I don't know them personally. I just know how concerned Matt's been about her."

Mrs. Rickles patted Kelly's arm. "I'll tell you what. You watch the desk for me, and I'll go see if there's any word about how things are going in there."

"Great! Thanks so much. But wait," she called as the volunteer started off down the hall. "What'll I do if someone asks for information or directions or something?"

"Stall 'em till I get back." Mrs. Rickles winked slyly over her shoulder. "Couldn't nothin' happen that Lucia St. Claire can't handle."

Reassured, Kelly stuck her hands in the pockets of her cranberry wool slacks and started wandering around the comfortable lobby. She tried to tell herself that once Mary's baby was safely born, Matt would be able to sleep better at night. Why couldn't he have specialized in something like podiatry or dermatology—something that wouldn't tear him apart? But would she love him if he didn't care so much?

Strolling into the gift shop, she absently fingered a crystal paperweight. She did love him. And Christmas was ten days away. What could she give him? She had plenty of money in the bank. She also had a sneaking suspicion that an expensive gift wouldn't impress Matt Kendall one iota.

Five minutes later as she stood in the hall studying the portraits of outstanding physicians who had served the hospital in the past, she heard footsteps behind her.

"Kelly."

"Matt!" She spun around, smiling. "Matt?" He looked awful—exhausted, bleak, anxious, preoccupied. His hair was a tangle of silvery blond curls from which he'd just yanked the surgical cap. He hadn't yet removed the wrinkled scrub greens. Even his shoes were still hidden beneath disposable coverings.

He seemed oddly distant as he stood there, his mouth tight, his shoulders slumped. Something must be terribly wrong.

"I can't take you to Lubbock," he said, his flat tone confirming her fear. "I'm sorry."

Disappointment formed a hot lump in her throat as she dwelled briefly on the trip that was not to be. The next instant she swallowed the lump and reached out to the man she loved. "I'm sorry, too, Matthew, but it's okay."

He walked into her arms and buried his face in the coppery cascade of her hair. Holding her close, he didn't speak, and Kelly found herself patting his broad back comfortingly. "Things didn't turn out quite the way you planned, did they?"

He shook his head and held her tighter.

"Is Mary okay?"

It took him a while to answer, and when he did his voice was low and hoarse. "I think she will be, eventually."

"The baby?"

The silence was even longer this time, and she could barely hear him. "There are . . . problems."

A chill climbed her spine. "What kind of problems?"

"His heart. Maybe his lungs, too. I don't know yet. The pediatrician is with him right now." He straightened slowly, reluctantly, but didn't release her. "I need to go back in there now. I told Dan I'd be there in case . . . just in case." The brown velvet softness of his eyes seemed cloudy as he focused on her upturned face. "Kelly, you go on to the game. Take my car—"

"Matt, forget the game." She didn't give a damn about the football game! "When you finish here, you just come on home to me. Do you hear? I'm going to fix a steak dinner for you."

He was shaking his head. "It may be late. I don't know when I'll get through."

"I don't care when you get through. You'd just better come," she said fiercely. "Or else!"

A tiny flicker deep in his eyes told her he was still capable of humor. "I hate to think what the 'or else' could be, ladychik. A stake through my heart?"

"At the very least." She squeezed, then released him and stepped back. "I'll be waiting."

At ten o'clock Kelly was still waiting, and Matt's steak was more than a trifle overdone. She started at every noise that might have been his car, strained to hear his step on the porch, then sank back against the sofa cushions in growing concern when his knock didn't come. What could be taking so long?

Any of a million complications, she knew. Matt would stay at the hospital until both mother and baby were out of danger.

Finally the telephone rang. She grabbed it up at once, certain it was Matt, but the voice on the other end was feminine.

"Miss West, this is Oleta Rickles from the hospital. I'm sorry to call you so late, but I thought I'd better find out if Dr. Kendall made it home all right."

Kelly's heart flipped over. "Isn't he at the hospital?"

"He left more than an hour ago, and considering the shape he was in, I just wanted to be sure he made it to your house." The older woman coughed delicately. "I, er, overheard you tell him to come."

"He hasn't arrived yet." Fighting panic, she recalled that last sound she'd heard, some time back. "Hold it a minute. Let me go look."

Peeking out the front window, she saw his white Blazer parked outside, lights and motor off. Kelly ran back to the phone. "He's here, Mrs. Rickles. I didn't hear him drive up. Just exactly what shape was he in when he left?"

"The Wilson baby died," Mrs. Rickles said simply, and Kelly needed no further explanation.

"Thank you for calling. I'll take care of him." Her eyes stung as she hung up.

She walked outside, too numb to notice the cold. Slowly crossing the lawn, she went straight to Matt's door and opened it. The faint light blinked on inside, showing him hunched forward with his arms folded over the steering wheel and his face pressed down on them. When she laid one hand on his shoulder, he lifted his head. Even in the dimness, his expression tore at her heart.

"Matthew," she said quietly, "why are you sitting out here? Come inside."

"I've been trying to, but...Kelly, I wouldn't be much company tonight. Maybe I'd better go on home."

Persuasively she took his hand and tried to warm it. "If you go home like this, you'll scare the wits out of your grandmother."

"You're right . . . I shouldn t go home. There's a place I can stay for a while . . ."

The cabin at the hunting lease that Rita had told Kelly about? There was no way Kelly was going to let Matt go there. Her fingers closed around his powerful wrist. "You come in my house right now, Matthew Kendall. I don't want to hear any argument about this."

Matt wasn't up to arguing. He looked vaguely at the slender, white-knuckled hand clenching his forearm and wondered why he didn't feel her grip. And if he couldn't feel *that*, how come the pain inside him was so real?

The next thing he knew, she was leading him into the house.

"Here, Matthew." She gestured at the living room sofa. Matt stood with his back to it, staring into the mesmerizing flames of the fireplace. "Sit down," she said, putting downward pressure on his shoulders. He sat.

Kelly shook her head and muttered to herself that he should have worn a coat. She sat down beside him and began rubbing his arms, terrified of the vacant expression that she'd never before seen in his dark eyes. He might be there physically, but the essence of Matthew Kendall was retreating from her faster than she could stop it.

She could think of only one way to reverse the process. "Tell me about it," she said. When he didn't respond, she repeated in a firm voice, "Tell me, Matt. What happened?"

With obvious effort he dragged his attention away from the fire and looked at her. "What?"

"Tell me what happened at the hospital."

At first he frowned as if he didn't understand her, but then the anguish began seeping back into his eyes. He ran a hand down his face and leaned back against the cushions. "Can't we just forget it for now?"

She studied him anxiously. He looked so tired, so beat. Heaven knows, she didn't want to hear about this any more than he wanted to tell her. "If I thought you'd really forget, Matthew, I wouldn't ask any questions," she said quietly. "But I know you better than that. Right now you're going inside yourself, somewhere in here—" she reached out and put her hands on either side of his head, plowing her fingers into his silky hair and clutching the curls tightly "—and you'll relive every second of this rotten afternoon over and over until you feel even worse than you do now, if that's possible."

His eyes focused on her in mute protest, but she ignored the plea that she read in them. "So," she concluded, "as long as you're going to go through it anyway, you're going to have to tell me about it. I want to know what it was like for you."

He drew a long, shuddering breath. "Oh, God, Kelly it was bad!"

He hadn't planned to say that. The words just seemed to slip out, and to his surprise he felt a modicum of relief. He'd never been able to share the pain before. He'd never even acknowledged to anyone that the pain existed. Super Doc, Luke mockingly called him. Pretend you can handle all the hard ones without flinching. Somehow he'd never quite managed that part of it.

Kelly didn't wait for him to volunteer the information. She touched him, and she made him talk. Just her nearness, her gentle persistence, opened a valve in him and started the words flowing, hesitantly at first.

"Mary was convinced she was going to be lucky this time. Unless you've watched someone go through six miscarriages, or been through them yourself, I guess it would be hard to understand how determined she was to have a baby. This was number seven. She thought we'd make it all the way home. She even had me believing it, too."

He spoke in a low voice. After listening closely for a moment, Kelly withdrew her fingers from his hair and curled up beside him, holding his hand.

"She wouldn't listen to reason. Every doctor in town told her to quit trying. *I* told her, but she's just so damnblasted stubborn!" His voice started to shake. "So strong and courageous. She would have made a good mother." Kelly felt his hand squeeze hers. He turned and looked straight into her worried green eyes, his own eyes filling with anger and confusion. "Brutus never had a chance!"

"Brutus?"

"The baby. He was going to be Dan Junior, but Mary called him Brutus. It was some kind of private joke between them that always made Dan laugh." Matt smiled fleetingly, then the weight of it all hit him again. "He had a heart defect, Kelly. Dammit, as if Mary's problems weren't enough, Brutus had to have a big one of his own!" His eyes filled with tears, and he pounded his thigh with his fist. "I hate this!"

Kelly grabbed his other hand to stop him and ended up putting her arms around him, holding him close. She felt his tears on her cheek and lifted her face to kiss his salty, silky, moist lashes. "What do you hate?"

"I hate it when the wrong people die. The babies, the ones who've never had a chance to live."

"You hate death."

"Oh, God, yes, I hate death!"

Her hands stroked up and down his back, soothing, massaging the tight corded muscles. "And so you fight it."

"With everything I've got! But it's not enough. I lose . . . too often."

"And sometimes you win."

He shuddered, starting to relax. "Yes," he admitted, "sometimes I win." He scooted sideways until he could stretch out full length on the sofa with her fragile softness molded against his long, hard form. Yawning tiredly, he said, "I wish I had won tonight."

"I wish you had too, Matthew."

For a long time Kelly lay watching the shadows of firelight flickering on the ceiling. She was afraid to move, hoping he'd fallen asleep, but when she did lift her head from his shoulder, she saw that his eyes were open.

"Does it always hit you this hard?" she murmured.

His head shifted toward her, and she thought he looked wary, defensive. "Not always. This was one of the worst." He frowned. "Look, I know what you're thinking. I should be able to handle this objectively. They taught us in med school not to get emotionally involved." Swallowing, he looked away. "Usually I manage, but sometimes . . . sometimes it's like my well has run dry. I just don't have the strength to stay cool. Or, in this case, I can't stop the feeling, no matter how hard I try."

She bent her head and brushed her lips over his. "Don't ever apologize for caring, Matt. It's one of the things that makes you so special."

He lay very still as a glowing warmth stole through him. "Am I special?"

"You're special," she assured him, her hand caressing his chest through the cotton fabric of his shirt. "Matthew Kendall, you are without a doubt the most incredibly special man I know. You're also a terrific doctor."

"So I'm not supposed to feel guilty about what happened today?"

"You did everything that was humanly possible. I don't know the medical details of the case, Matt, but that much I do know. You're the best doctor in town, and Mary Wilson was lucky to have you taking care of her." Kelly spoke levelly. "Don't you *ever* question the truth of that, do you hear?" Then she added simply, "I would trust you with my life."

It was exactly what he needed to hear.

Ten minutes later he was sound asleep in Kelly's bed, and soon afterward she joined him, sneaking close to his body for warmth and the tangible reassurance that he was there. She'd offered to feed him first, but he said one of the nurses had brought him a sandwich earlier in the evening and he just wasn't hungry. Thinking about that charred T-bone in the kitchen, Kelly figured it was just as well.

She was surprised the next morning to wake up to a warm house and the delicious aroma of bacon and biscuits. According to the clock, it was eight A.M. and Matt was still there!

In a flash, she was out of bed, thrusting her arms into a robe and tearing down the hall to find him.

Showered, shaved and dressed, he stood at the stove, forking at least a pound of crisp bacon strips out of the frying pan and onto a pad of paper napkins. Kelly noted the huge platter of scrambled eggs and the dozen hot biscuits he'd already buttered. "Can I assume you're hungry now?" she asked dryly.

Matt turned. "Starved! I'm afraid I just emptied your refrigerator."

She shrugged. "Don't worry. I don't cook if I can help it. I eat out most of the time."

Spearing the blackened remains of last night's steak and holding it up, he grinned at her. "I think I can see why."

Kelly accepted his teasing with good nature, delighted to find him looking so much better. As she set the table, she observed casually, "You don't often sleep this late, do you?"

"No." For a second he glanced away from her. Then he met her eyes again and took a long breath. "When my internal alarm clock went off at four this morning, I did a lot of thinking . . . about . . . things. About how sometimes I wish I could hide out somewhere for a week or two until I can put things back into perspective. About how good it would feel to sleep until seven some morning." A trace of a smile tugged at the corners of his sensual mouth. "About the lady who was all wrapped around me, keeping me warm. I knew I didn't really want to get out of bed just then. So I didn't." He tilted his chin up rather defiantly, as if he expected Kelly, or perhaps the AMA, to chastise him.

"Good for you," she said, thinking it was high time he started living like a human being. "And did you sleep till seven?"

"Six-forty-five." He still seemed to feel a need to excuse himself. "Gerry McKettrick had already agreed to cover for me this weekend, so I thought maybe we could spend a couple of days together. If you're not busy."

She whooped in delight and dropped the silverware, throwing her arms around his waist and scattering the biscuits he was carrying in every direction. "You mean it?" she demanded, laughing up at him. He looked so wonderful, she thought, his brown eyes a little bemused by her enthusiasm but warm and happy as he hugged her back.

Kelly savored every single minute of the weekend. After breakfast, they went back to bed, where they made slow, leisurely, satisfying love and then napped until noon when they woke up and made love again.

That afternoon they drove to Dallas and did some Christmas shopping. Matt demonstrated a flair for picking out the most original and appropriate gifts for his family, a knack that probably resulted from his perceptive observation of those he loved. Kelly asked him to advise her when it came to her own purchases for the Kendalls, and he did so willingly. Only when she asked what she should get Luke John did he flounder.

"I have no idea what he'd like," Matt said, impatiently picking out a shirt and proceeding to the next person on the list. To Kelly it seemed that he hadn't given much thought to his brother's taste, but when she tried to draw him out on the subject, he proved just how evasive he could be. And when mistaken for his famous twin in three different stores, he coldly denied being Luke John Kendall and silenced the autograph hounds with a scathing glare, totally out of character for Matt. Again he refused to discuss it with Kelly.

They talked about almost everything else, though and what they couldn't agree upon, they debated, their mutual respect growing by the hour. Kelly almost confided in him that she had a lunch date with Phillip Farnsworth on Tuesday to talk about a job, but she decided to save the news for Christmas, if it worked out.

After eating dinner in Dallas, they drove back to Weatherford, and Matt stopped by the hospital, saying he needed to see Mary Wilson for a moment. Kelly guessed that he wanted to tell her, now that she was fully conscious, how very sorry he was about the baby.

He returned to Kelly in the lobby looking thoughtful and at peace with himself, and she wished she could have thanked the grieving but wise lady who had evidently freed him from any self-blame.

They talked then about babies—about children—and Kelly admitted she wanted a dozen.

Matt laughed. "You'd better get started then. They do take time to develop."

She considered cracking a joke, something to the effect that she was now interviewing prospects for the father of her children, but she wasn't sure how Matt would react. The topic of marriage hadn't come up in their conversation thus far.

When Kelly remained silent, he said, no longer laughing, "I'd like a handful of kids myself, but I'm afraid of shortchanging them. I'm so busy, I don't know when I'd spend any time with them."

At least it gave her the opportunity to say, "I can see you need a lot more practice at this weekend-off business. Fear not, I'm a good teacher."

"That's not all you're good at," he murmured, giving her a look that was so potent, she felt the resulting tingle right down to her toes.

So much for philosophical discussions. As soon as they arrived at Kelly's house, they began working their way toward the bedroom, shedding clothes as they went, and ended up in each other's arms again, in bed, in absolute rapture. Kelly's heart swelled with her love for Matt, even more so when he cradled her against him afterward and chuckled softly. "If I tell you something, will you swear you won't laugh?"

"*You're* laughing!"

"That's different. I'm allowed to laugh. But you have to promise not to. My feelings might get hurt."

"All right, I promise."

His finger trailed lightly over the bare skin of her abdomen, sketching a feathery line of fire everywhere he touched. "When you were sixteen years old," he said slowly, "I wanted to ask you for a date."

Her eyes widened. "You did?"

Nodding, he said, "One semester in particular—remember when we had study hall together and you sat in front of me—I came very close."

"Well, what stopped you?"

Grinning crookedly, he looked up at her for a moment, then dropped his eyes again. "You were otherwise occupied."

"You mean Luke? But that was all in my head! Ahhhh, Matt... you should have asked!"

He wondered if she would have accepted back then, but he just said, "Well, it makes for interesting speculation, anyway," and tried to change the subject.

Kelly persisted. "Where would you have taken me?"

"Oh, I don't know. I never planned that far ahead. The movies, probably. And then parking," he added with a wicked leer.

Kelly threw back her head and laughed. "It's really too bad you didn't ask me, Matthew. I'd have loved to have gone parking with a hunk like you."

"You would?" Even though he didn't believe her, he didn't care to push it. The present was too perfect to spoil by dissecting the past. "It's not too late, you know. We can still park and neck and... everything." He lowered his head and caught her nipple between his teeth, sparking an electric need in her that sizzled along her nerve endings like lightning.

"Where?" she gasped. "When?"

"Mmmm, I don't know. We'll find a place," he whispered. "Meet me at the Dairy Bar. Eleven o'clock. New Year's Eve. We'll go from there." He kissed the smooth plane of her belly. "We can ring in the New Year together."

"Oh, yes!" she breathed, arching in exquisite agony. "Together!"

On Sunday he took her to church, stopping at the Christmas tree lot on the way home and buying a six-foot fir tree, which they set up in Kelly's living room. She wanted to decorate it at once, but he said the tree trimming would just have to wait until evening as they were already late for Sunday dinner at the Kendall place.

During the noisy and thoroughly delightful meal, they received a blow-by-blow account of the Kangaroos' close defeat by Lubbock Monterey in the regional finals. After dinner, Matt and Kelly drove to the oak-ridged hill near the eastern boundary of the Kendall ranch, and Matt showed her the spot where he planned to build his own home someday.

The view was spectacular, conveying such a sense of vast space and peace. "You must be so excited, Matthew. When will you start construction?"

He didn't sound excited. "Oh . . . there's no rush." He stared out over the gently rolling countryside, frowning at his thoughts. She guessed that he was thinking about his grandmother's growing dependence and his own decision to try to keep her out of a rest home. Kelly would have given anything at that moment to be able to tell him she loved him and wanted to share his problems, but he'd never mentioned love, or commitment, or even living together.

Standing in the weak December sunshine on the grassy crest of the hill, he took her face between his hands and kissed her with such tenderness that she almost blurted her words of love, whether ill-advised or not. Wrapping her in his strong arms, he crushed her to him with something that felt very much like desperation. "Thank you, Kelly."

His husky tone bothered her. He sounded so somber. "For what?"

"For this weekend." He couldn't put into words all she had done for him, the miraculous healing she'd wrought. He couldn't tell her what she meant to him. Not now.

"You're welcome." It was an effort to hide her frustration. Didn't he know they had a lifetime ahead of them, that there would be many other weekends for them to share?

But Matt wasn't thinking of future weekends. At the moment he was trying to shut his mind to all thought of the future because of something his father had told him after dinner.

Luke John was coming home on Friday.

10

KELLY PROPPED HER CHIN ON HER HAND as she sat in the back corner booth at the Dairy Bar, aimlessly stirring her coffee, watching Millie hang tinsel garlands and strings of colored lights. She started to ask why Millie had waited until Christmas Eve to decorate the restaurant—and why she was bothering to decorate at all since Kelly was the only customer in the place—but then she sighed and kept silent. If she gave Millie another opening, the waitress would chatter all afternoon, and Kelly needed to think instead. She had a lot to think about.

The job offer, for instance. At lunch on Tuesday Mr. Farnsworth had made an excellent case for her coming to work at the college. Kelly liked the idea of producing four plays each year, including a musical in the summer. She could see any number of points in favor of her accepting the job. At the same time, she didn't want to make a decision without talking it over with Matt first. But that was the problem—she suddenly couldn't talk to Matt about *anything*.

Frowning, she plunked her spoon down on the table and took a sip of the coffee. Cold. Terrific. Just about as cold as Matt had been treating her for the past week.

She couldn't pinpoint his problem, but she had noticed last Sunday that he was acting peculiar. While decorating her Christmas tree, he'd seemed unusually preoccupied and had made an early night of it. Since then he'd been too busy to see her. He had called only once, on Wednesday evening, and then had spoken to her for all of two minutes before excusing himself, saying his beeper had just gone off and he needed to call his service. She had got the feeling that he hadn't really wanted to call in the first place.

Bewildered, she asked herself what was going on. Was he up to his ears in work, as he said? If so, what was he doing eating lunch in the hospital cafeteria on Friday with Angela Guest? Didn't he know that if he'd called Kelly and had invited her to lunch, she'd have dropped everything and come running?

The thought made her squirm. Kelly didn't like to feel at a man's mercy, even if the man *was* Matthew Kendall. Even if she *did* love him. She was accustomed to functioning independently. It was a totally new experience for her to spend the better part of a week slaving over a Christmas present for a man, and she felt slightly foolish now for having done so. Studying the needle pricks in her finger, she wondered if Matt would even appreciate the thought behind her gift. Probably not. Just as he hadn't appreciated her and Jenny dropping by the hospital at noon on Friday to remind him that Luke was arriving that afternoon and that Rita expected Matt to join them for a celebration supper at the ranch.

Looking up at Kelly as if she had had no business tracking him down during a tête-à-tête with Angela, he had informed them in a quiet voice that he would certainly try to come.

To the dismay of everyone, he had never shown up. Despite Luke John's barbed comments about the good doctor being too busy to welcome his brother home, Kelly had sensed that Luke was really hurt at Matt's absence. As for herself, she had felt angry and embarrassed, and it hadn't helped that Rita and Jenny were furious with him on her behalf.

Kelly wished everyone would just butt out. Couldn't they all see what was becoming more and more clear to her—that a couple of dates and a weekend spent with Kelly were not enough to erase the memory of Matt's marriage, and that Kelly could never hope to measure up to Meredith.

The door opened and closed, pulling Kelly back to the present just as Millie chirped gaily from atop her stepladder, "Merry Christmas! I'll be right with you!"

"No hurry." The voice was sexy, amused and painfully familiar, and Kelly's head jerked up. When she saw the tall blond hunk heading straight for her, her heart did a crazy flip before it resumed its normal rhythm.

"Hello," she muttered.

"Hey, I deserve at least a hug," Luke John Kendall protested, slipping into the booth beside her and nudging her over with his hip. He slid an arm across her shoulders and squeezed. "Didn't anyone tell you it's Christmas Eve?"

Kelly frowned. "Merry Christmas."

He laughed. "That sounded more like 'Bah, humbug' than 'Merry Christmas.'" When Millie appeared at his elbow, beaming, he beamed right back at her and ordered a cup of coffee for himself and a refill for Kelly. "Business is a little slow, isn't it?" he observed.

"I know how we can fix that," Millie said, eyes sparkling.

"Uh-uh," Luke said, still laughing. "Not this time."

"All I have to do," Millie explained as if both Kelly and Luke hadn't already figured it out, "is stand outside on the street corner and tell people Luke John Ken-dall is having a banana split at the Dairy Bar. It'd fill the place up in sixty seconds flat." She winked. "I'll throw in the split on the house."

"You ought to throw it in anyway," Luke chided her, "after I gave your redheaded pal an interview the other day."

On the way home from the airport on Friday, Jenny had seen Kelly's BMW parked at the Dairy Bar and had stopped and brought Luke inside to say hello. Once again, Millie had summoned Bo Hanover and this time the aggressive young TV cameraman had captured Luke John Kendall and Kelly West together on tape for the six o'clock news. Still stunned from seeing Matt with Angela, Kelly had been sufficiently defiant to put on a good show for the audience, playing up the kissy-kissy Hollywood version of friend meeting long-lost friend. Well, she *was* glad to see Luke, but she'd have been a heck of a lot more enthusiastic about kissing his twin.

"How'd we look on TV?" she asked idly, not having bothered to watch it herself.

"We looked great!" Millie announced, enormously pleased with the way she'd maneuvered herself into the spotlight twice in as many weeks. "Everybody loved us!" She departed to get the coffee, thinking what a shame it was that she couldn't head for Hollywood herself.

Luke still had his arm around Kelly, and as soon as Millie had brought two steaming cups and gone away again, he bent his head to peer into her face. "If this is what two weeks in Weatherford does to you, I hope you get on back to L.A. where you belong."

For once he sounded serious and concerned. He sounded like Matt would have sounded a week ago. "I belong here. This is my home."

"Then what's the problem?"

I only wish I knew, she thought, shaking her head and shrugging.

"You and Matt!" Luke withdrew his arm and slid down low in the seat, looking disgruntled. "You make a fine pair. Both of you grouches. Both of you claiming you'll be happy to stay here the rest of your lives."

Kelly didn't know how happy she'd be now that Matt didn't have time for her, but she wasn't going to turn tail and run so soon. "How did your reunion with Matthew go?" she asked, to change the subject.

He didn't answer for a minute, and when he did his voice was low, his brown eyes fixed on the table in front of him. "About as usual. I should have known it would be a mistake for me to come home again."

All of a sudden Luke sounded really depressed, and Kelly blinked in shock. Luke the charmer, the superstar, never gave a hint that everything in his life wasn't in divinely blessed order. He had an image to project.

Fleetingly Kelly remembered the twins as they had been in high school—intelligent, talented, well-liked each in his own way, and, for all their personal differences, inseparable.

"Luke, what happened between you two?"

He shoved his hands into the pockets of his jeans and looked as if he regretted his temporary lapse. "Nothing."

"Funny. That's exactly what Matt said when I asked him that same question, and I didn't believe him either."

He sat up abruptly and faced her. "You asked Matt what happened? Why?"

"Because of the way he acts whenever anyone mentions you."

His mouth twisted. "As if he hates me?" Seeing her startled expression, he said, "Hey, it's okay. I've gotten used to it by now."

"I don't know about hate. The truth is, he acts almost jealous of you."

"Jealous!" Luke snorted. "Why should he be jealous?"

"He shouldn't," Kelly said so bluntly that he grinned at her jab. "Just for the record, Matt makes our lives—yours and mine—seem about as significant as sugar frosting on a gingerbread house. Seriously," she insisted when Luke's expression turned mocking. "We could drop out of sight tomorrow and it wouldn't affect anyone for long. I did already, remember, and the world just went right on spinning. Oh, sure, six million screaming teenyboppers would wonder what happened to Luke John Kendall until some other handsome sexpot came along to take your place. But Matt's different. His contributions are the kind that last. When he goes, he'll be truly missed."

Luke fidgeted, frowning. "Just what's the point of all this? To let me know you've fallen in love with Matt? You're too late. Everyone else in the family's already told me."

A flush crept up her throat to her cheeks. "We weren't talking about my feelings for Matt."

"No, we weren't. So maybe you just wanted to be sure I know how I compare to my paragon of a brother? Don't worry. Whenever I come home, there are twelve thousand people right here in Weatherford who are more than happy to remind me. All I hear, all over town, is what a saint Matt is."

She gaped. "*You're* jealous? You're actually jealous of Matt!"

"No, I'm not. I'm damned proud of him." Luke spoke softly, the sarcasm gone from his voice. "I wish I had a few of his sterling qualities. I wish—"

He broke off when someone came in to order. For a while there was a steady stream of customers, all of them apparently travelers in a rush to get home for Christmas. After the first one stared curiously at Luke and Kelly, Luke got up and moved to the seat facing her, putting his back to the door, and from then on no one paid them any attention.

"When did you and Matt have your, um, falling out?" Kelly asked.

He glanced up sharply. "We didn't. We never disagreed on anything. Nothing that mattered, anyway. He just . . . I don't know what happened, Kelly, although it all seems to go back to Meredith's death."

Meredith Kendall was the last person in the world Kelly wanted to talk about on Christmas Eve, but with a sort of horrible fascination she heard herself ask, "How well did you know her?"

"Not very well. I only met her once." Luke explained that because he hadn't been able to attend the wedding, Matt and Meredith had spent two days of their honeymoon with him in New York City, where he was starring in his second feature film. "She was a beautiful girl. That's just what she was—a kid. Her father was an oilman who had sent her to all the best schools, but for all that she was pretty impressionable. She couldn't get over the fact that I was a movie star." There was another trace of self-mockery in his brief smile. "I got the feeling Meredith was accustomed to getting everything she wanted, and I figured Matt was going to have his hands full keeping her happy."

"I hope you didn't make the mistake of saying so to him. Is *that* the connection between her death and Matt's problem with you?"

Luke looked at her as if she'd grown another head. "I'm not a total idiot. Of course I didn't tell my brother he'd married a spoiled brat. Besides, I don't really know if there is a connection. I only know that when I returned home after the funeral he didn't call me anymore, and when I called him he acted remote. Before she died, I'd invited them to come see me, and Matt wanted to come, or at least he said he did. Afterward, he wouldn't even talk about it."

Kelly tapped the tip of a fingernail against her coffee mug absently, thinking about Luke's words. "But his attitude toward the rest of the family didn't change when she was killed. Why would he start treating you differently?"

"I don't know, dammit!" Averting his head, Luke spoke roughly, as if to disguise the emotion in his voice. "I don't understand anything about my brother anymore. Why does he think he has to live like a monk?" Kelly bit her tongue to keep from informing him that Matt hadn't exactly taken a vow of chastity. "Why does he insist on punishing himself . . . wasting his life?"

"Like the man in your song, you mean? Luke, don't you think it's rather mercenary of you to cash in on Matt's tragedy by singing about it?"

"Cash in on it!" He jerked his head back and scowled at Kelly, but she saw a suspicious moistness on his lashes that stunned her. Luke John Kendall had tears in his eyes! "Is that what you think? Is that what he thinks?"

"I don't know what Matt thinks." She started to tell him that Matt had probably never even listened to his latest record, but Luke went on before she got a chance.

"I wanted to make him see what he's doing to himself. That's all. I just wanted him to stop and think about where he's headed. Is her memory worth the loneliness? He's my brother . . . my best friend. At least he used to be. It's almost as if he died. And I miss him. Lord help me, I miss him!" Luke's voice came dangerously near to breaking, and when Kelly reached out and took his hand he gripped hers with bone-crushing intensity. "All I wanted was for him to listen to my song— to really listen. I only sang it for him, Kelly. I'd give everything I've got if he'd just put his arms around me and tell me he understands what I've been trying to say to him. But you know something? I don't think there's a chance in hell that he ever will."

Responding to Luke's grief, Kelly moved over to sit beside him, hugging him in silent sympathy. She knew how he felt. With every passing hour, it seemed less likely that her relationship with Matt could survive.

MATT LEFT THE HOSPITAL and cut over to Main Street, heading toward the center of town. He planned to stop by his office and catch up on some more paperwork before going home. Then he'd have to rush if he hoped to get cleaned up and make it to the ranch in time for tonight. The Kendalls always had their tree on Christmas Eve. It was one of the few family traditions he'd managed to participate in consistently since he had opened his practice, and he was thinking seriously of skipping tonight. One miss in four years wouldn't be a bad track record.

For a minute he wavered, thinking about Rita and Tom's pleasure at having the entire family together for Christmas for the first time in eight years.

Then he thought about Kelly being there, because of course she would be. These days she was as much a part of the family as he was. Picturing the way she would look at Luke—the same way she'd looked at him on the six o'clock news Friday night—he felt his chest tighten until he could hardly breathe.

From the moment he had learned that Luke was coming home, Matt's imagination had had a field day, convincing him Kelly was fated to fall back in love with Luke. They were too much alike. Seeing no point in postponing the inevitable, Matt had begun at once to pull out of her life so that he might at least salvage his pride when Kelly realized it was Luke John she still wanted. All her talk about staying in Weatherford forever had been just that—talk. If she'd been serious, she would have accepted Phil Farnsworth's job offer. But she'd never even mentioned the job to Matt, who had heard about it from the banker himself.

For all his vivid imaginings, when he had seen that newsclip of Kelly throwing her arms around Luke and returning his enthusiastic kiss, Matt had known he hadn't really prepared himself. It was happening faster than he had expected, and he couldn't handle the pain. After that, he couldn't have faced Luke's welcome-home dinner, even if the alternative had been a firing squad, so he'd stayed away. When he did finally see Luke on Saturday, it was a short, cool meeting, bearable only because Kelly wasn't there.

This morning Jenny had skipped church to confront him at his office. "You watched that ridiculous thing on TV Friday night, didn't you?" she said. "Ah, Matt, you know how Luke is. He kisses every female in sight, especially when there's a television camera trained on him. It doesn't mean a thing."

Yes, Matt knew how Luke was. The problem wasn't Luke; it was Kelly's feelings for Luke.

When he had asked Jenny to please mind her own business, she had told him, sounding exasperated, that he *was* her business. "I have an obligation to point out how dumb you're acting. Go talk to Kelly if you don't believe me. She doesn't care about Luke that way anymore. She outgrew her crush on him a long time ago."

Sure. And Matt had the Nobel prize for medicine in his hip pocket.

He wouldn't listen, and Jenny had left in angry tears, calling him a fool. Well, maybe he was one, but the whole town didn't have to know it. He would pretend he didn't mind when Luke and Kelly flaunted their... their affair, or whatever it could be called, for everyone to see.

Somewhere deep inside him Matt nurtured a tiny doubt that Kelly would actually go to bed with Luke after sharing herself with Matt the past two weeks. So when he saw her BMW at the Dairy Bar, he slammed on his brakes and stopped, too nervous to notice his mother's car at the other end of the parking lot. Kelly was there. He would ask her.

He got as far as the door when he looked in and saw them. Kelly and Luke were sitting with their backs to the window. They were holding each other, their heads close together. And there wasn't a TV camera in the place. This was reality.

Matt turned and walked slowly back to his Blazer.

"I THINK I'D BETTER SKIP TONIGHT," Kelly said as Luke walked her out to her car. "You Kendalls have some private things to work out."

He gave a resigned sigh. "They won't get worked out tonight, honey. And if you tell anyone . . ." He leveled a threatening scowl at her, and she just shook her head and hugged him again. The big dope. He thought it would tarnish his image if word got out that Luke John Kendall was human.

"I hope one day Matt will let you in on what's bothering him. I love you both."

"Yeah? Well, I appreciate your love, even if my saintly brother doesn't." He opened the car door for her and then stood staring down at her, a slow smile dawning as he entertained a brainstorm. "What you need is to make ol' Matthew jealous."

"No, I don't think—"

"Yes! Brilliant!" He patted her cheek. "Don't you worry about a thing. Just leave it up to me."

"I don't know, Luke, really—"

"You just come on over. What time did Mom tell you?"

"Seven."

"Right. See you at seven. Oh, Kelly," he called as she shut her door. "Come as Lucia tonight, hmm?" Still grinning, he waved her off.

Kelly wasn't convinced that Luke's idea would work, whatever his idea was. She'd probably be wiser to stay away from Matt. But she needed to deliver her presents, and besides, Rita and Grandma would be hurt if she didn't show up.

It took her two hours to get ready. For some reason she obeyed Luke's odd request and decked herself out in green taffeta, the only party dress that hadn't gone under the knife. It was a slinky designer gown, which combined with her skillfully applied makeup and exotic perfume, transformed her into Lucia St. Claire in the flesh. Her copper-colored hair swept over one shoulder in a torrent of glossy waves, and her skin glowed like golden honey. The shawl she wore matched the gown but did little to shield her from the chilly night air.

Upon her arrival at the huge, warm, brightly lit ranch house, Luke John and Tom and Bill Lewis made a big deal of standing in line to kiss the notorious villainess, and Lisa and Rita teased the men unmercifully about their lust. While it was all very flattering, it wasn't likely to make Matt jealous, Kelly thought dryly, since Matt wasn't there. Neither was Jenny.

Tom popped corn in the fireplace to go with Rita's hot apple cider, and Lisa persuaded Luke to sing Christmas carols for the mostly appreciative audience. Grandma dropped off to sleep in her chair almost immediately, and Bill had to apologize repeatedly for his two small sons who kept running to the front door to look out and ask how much longer Santa Claus was going to be.

Although no one offered any explanations, it soon became apparent to Kelly that everyone was stalling. When, an hour later, Jenny escorted an unsmiling Matt inside and Bill muttered, "Praise the Lord," Kelly guessed that Jenny must have had the very devil of a time either finding her brother or persuading him to come out to the ranch.

As if on cue, Luke strolled over to Kelly and put his arm around her, and Bill snagged the children's attention. "Sshh! Bobby, Andy—listen! Do you hear that? Sleigh bells!"

Lisa got into the act. "I think I hear reindeer on the roof," she confided in a stage whisper. "Let's go up and see if we can spot them."

The trusting little souls each took one of her hands and scampered up the stairs. The moment they were out of sight, their parents began opening closets and whipping out what looked like the entire inventory of two toy stores.

After five minutes, Lisa and the boys ran back downstairs, the older one shouting, "I saw him! I saw Santa flying away! He had on a cowboy hat like Grandpa, and he was smoking a big cigar."

"Active imagination," Luke whispered in Kelly's ear. "I like that kid. He's going to be a terrific actor someday."

Kelly had to smile. Luke was really pouring it on thick. The way he was looking at her, he could eat her up with his eyes, and he was murmuring sweet nothings about his five-year-old nephew.

It all seemed to be wasted on Matt, who sat staring into the fire, toying with the mug of cider Rita had put into his hand.

The boys' hyperactivity level escalated, if possible, when they discovered the loot under the tree, and for the next hour everyone was occupied opening gifts and shouting approval and thanks back and forth across the room. While Matt didn't shout, he did make some effort to appear grateful for his presents.

Halfway down her own stack, Kelly came to a beautifully wrapped package and read the tag thoughtfully.

"To Kelly West from Matt Kendall." Coolly impersonal and definitely not in his handwriting. With a feeling of dread, she opened it and stared at the flagon of expensive perfume. It was perfect for Lucia, and it was totally wrong for Kelly.

Lifting her eyes, she inadvertently met Matt's gaze before she had a chance to put on a pleased facade. "I can see you don't share Angela's taste in perfume," he said into the unfortunate silence that fell just then. "Cheer up. You can always exchange it."

Everyone heard his remark, so they all had to draw the same conclusion as Kelly: he had asked his receptionist to buy something for Kelly.

For once pretending was beyond her. Too hurt to speak, she blinked and swallowed and hurriedly left the room.

To Matt's horror, the yawning silence stretched as he watched the vivid figure in green almost run out the door. He half rose to follow her, but Luke beat him to it, muttering, "I'd better see about Kelly."

Matt slumped back in his chair, feeling awful. What had come over him to hurt her deliberately like that? Shaking, he ran a hand over his eyes and glanced around at the rest of his family, who were looking anywhere but at him.

He started to push aside his presents and then realized that he had one more to open. It was wrapped in the brightest green paper he'd ever seen, with a bow made of red yarn tied around it. He unfolded the accompanying card and felt his heart turn over. Kelly had written in her forthright scrawl, "One of these days you'll have your dream home, Matthew. When you do, please hang this where you can see it every day and know that I mean it. Merry Christmas with love, Kelly."

Something told Matt he wasn't going to like himself any better after he opened this present. Fingers trembling, he untied the bow and tore off the wrapping, then lifted the lid of the box. Inside, wrapped in tissue paper, was an oak-framed sampler embroidered in small, even stitches, leafy green vines entwined around the border. Across the center, blue cross-stitched letters spelled out Kelly's message: "If your well runs dry, drink from mine."

Matt closed his eyes, his stomach churning with confused misery. Oh, hell. He hadn't intended to hurt her. He'd only made that nasty comment because he was hurting so much himself.

Maybe I've been wrong, he thought. *Maybe Kelly really cares about me.* When he lifted his head and saw Kelly and Luke come back into the room arm in arm, Matt amended that to past tense. Maybe she *had* cared. Matt had given her little reason to care this past week.

Grandma, who had been dozing in her corner, roused herself just then to ask why everyone had gotten so quiet.

"We're all tired, I imagine," Rita said, rocking Andy in her arms. "Are you ready to go to bed, Mama?"

"Soon." Annie nodded. "Soon. But while we're all together, I think it's time I made an announcement."

She was looking at Matt so seriously that he tried to shove aside the jumbled chaos in his head and concentrate on his grandmother. Leaning forward, he watched her gnarled blue-veined hands as they gently stroked the afghan covering her lap.

"I always said I wouldn't move in with my kids." She flicked a glance at her daughter, who didn't look surprised. "Always wanted to be independent. To die in my own bed at home. Lately I've come to see there are some things more important than being independent. That's why I'm accepting Tom and Rita's invitation to come stay with them."

Matt stared at Grandma in astonishment. Jenny and Lisa had tears in their eyes, but they seemed to approve of her decision. Luke was watching Matt, his expression inscrutable.

"It'll be easier on everyone if I move out here," Annie continued calmly. "My mind is eighty-six years old. Sometimes it plays tricks on me. 'Course, my body ain't exactly spry, either. I need a little more help than I used to. Then there's Matt." Annie's cloudy eyes wandered back to her grandson. "He'll be needing some privacy now that he's marrying Kelly."

A stunned silence swept the room. No one dared look at Matt or Kelly.

"I've imposed long enough," the old lady concluded, "and I thank you, Matthew Mark Kendall, for these four years you've given me. I thank you from the bottom of my grateful old heart."

"Grandma," he began, then cleared his throat. "Grandma, you aren't imposing. I enjoy sharing your house—"

"Grandma," Luke John cut in with a cool look at his brother, "there's no need for you to jump the gun here. I don't know where you got the idea that Kelly's marrying Matt. I've just about got her convinced to fly back to L.A. with me for a New Year's Eve party my producer is throwing. I want her to be in my next film."

This was the first Kelly had heard of Luke's plans for her, but she just shut her eyes and leaned her head back against the sofa cushions, too drained to react. She didn't have the strength or the motivation to correct the impression Luke was giving everyone. If anyone believed she was still tempted by Hollywood, they obviously didn't know her very well.

As soon as she could without seeming rude, Kelly gathered up her things and announced that she had to go. Luke and Bill carried her presents out to the car while she kissed the others good-night. When she got to Matt, she aimed a brittle smile in his general direction and shook his hand. "Thanks for the perfume."

"Kelly..." He held on to her hand, and she forced herself to meet his gaze. She'd never seen his dark eyes so troubled. Good! She hoped he felt so guilty that he wouldn't be able to sleep a wink tonight.

"Yes, Matt?"

His voice was very low, very hoarse. "I like the...the gift you made for me. You did make it, didn't you?" He was looking at her closely, as if her answer mattered to him.

She concentrated on keeping her voice from shaking. "Don't mention it." She wasn't kidding. If he ever mentioned her sampler again, she would pick it up and smash it, frame and all, over his beautiful blond head. Pulling her hand free, she turned and walked away.

AFTER THE CHRISTMAS EVE DISASTER, Kelly certainly didn't intend to return to the scene of the crime for Christmas dinner, but the next morning Jenny and Bill came and practically kidnapped her. They paid not a bit of attention to her outraged protests, and she finally decided to go quietly in a semidignified manner.

It turned out to be a better day than she had expected. Matt didn't come, and Luke didn't pretend to be madly in love with her. Somehow she managed not to spend more than six hours daydreaming about Matt, thanks to endless games of Trivial Pursuit and more food than even Kelly could safely consume in one day.

The subsequent days weren't so easy. Everyone was too busy to sit around keeping Kelly's mind off her troubles. Everyone except Luke John, that is, and it didn't help much to have a mirror image of Matt constantly turning up on her doorstep. Still, he was an old friend, and they shared a powerful common denominator—a raw sense that Matt had deserted them without cause.

With each passing day that Matt didn't call, Kelly's hope shriveled up a little more. She wanted to cry, to get rid of the tears that burned behind her eyelids, but she was afraid to let go. Once started, the tears would probably never stop. Anyway, what she really wanted to do was to confront Matt, to demand a reason for his behavior. But that her pride would not allow.

When Jenny told her Matt wouldn't make a move because he thought there was something going on between Kelly and Luke, Kelly said that was a cowardly cop-out, that Matt would just rather not give up his unhealthy attachment to Meredith. And she thought, feeling suddenly reckless, *You want to see something between Luke and me? Just hide and watch, Matthew Kendall!*

For the last three days that Luke was in town, Kelly occupied most of his time. They went dancing in Fort Worth, and at the White Elephant Saloon Luke took Kelly up on stage with him to belt out a couple of his biggest hit songs for the screaming fans. The impromptu performance made the front page of the *Fort Worth Star Telegram* and the caption beneath the picture read as if Kelly and Luke John were an item.

The next day she reaped an unexpected benefit from the newspaper story when the director of the Casa Mañana theater in Fort Worth called to ask if Kelly would be interested in signing a contract to play the lead in several productions during the next year. She agreed to think it over.

Bo Hanover pursued Kelly and Luke around Weatherford until she finally agreed to one more joint interview. This time he positioned them in front of the bronze statue of Mary Martin's Peter Pan that posed impishly on the lawn of the public library. Bo got Luke to talk about the movie he'd just completed, then asked if there was any truth to the rumor that Kelly would be going back to Hollywood with Luke.

He looked at Kelly and smiled. "Ahhh . . . that's not for publication just yet." Her eyes filled up with bitter tears as she realized Matt wouldn't care if she went. Luke pulled her to him for a hug, kissed her bright wind-tousled hair and whispered something in her ear, and the camera caught it all—all except his words, which weren't the least bit romantic. He was telling her to keep her chin up, hang in there, stiff upper lip and all that.

The next day Luke was gone. Rita asked Kelly to drive with the family to see him off at the airport, but she declined. It was New Year's Eve, and she needed some time alone. That afternoon she tramped the pasture and fields of her farm for hours thinking about the events of the past few weeks. She had come back to Texas to make a quiet country life for herself. She could still have that life, only somehow it didn't seem to be enough any longer. She needed more. She needed Matt.

If she hadn't run into him that first day...if she hadn't spent all that time with him and come to know the very special man that he was inside…if only she hadn't fallen in love so deeply, so hopelessly! But she had, and now she knew exactly what was going to be missing from her life without him.

And she might have blown this herself. Jenny had tried to tell her that Matt was jealous of Luke, but Kelly had responded by flaunting herself with Luke. How had that made Matt feel?

Torn with doubts, Kelly trudged back to her house. What if Jenny was right? What if Matt loved her? He had made a date to meet her tonight, but a lot had happened since then. Was it too late?

Kelly got out the telephone directory and made a couple of phone calls, pulling every string within her reach, then took a long, hot bath and tried to relax. At ten o'clock she was dressed again and sitting in front of the television with her fingers crossed.

Sure enough, the news anchorman headlined the evening's broadcast with a story about Kelly West being officially named as the new head of the drama department at Weatherford College. In announcing the appointment, Phillip Farnsworth praised Kelly's background and experience and dismissed as ridiculous the rumor that she had already decided to return to Hollywood. "Miss West assured me when we talked this afternoon that she loves the people of Weatherford," Mr. Farnsworth said, and Kelly thought, *Listen, Matt! Please hear what I'm trying to tell you.* "She looks forward to a long and happy life here in the community where her heart is."

She noted with satisfaction that the banker had quoted her perfectly. Now if only Matt had been watching….

THERE WERE HALF A DOZEN CARS at the Dairy Bar when Kelly arrived at ten-fifty, but Matt's Blazer wasn't among them. *Don't panic,* she told herself. *He still has ten minutes.*

What if he didn't come? The possibility existed and should be faced, but Kelly opted for confidence. She slid the red BMW into one of several empty slots in front so that Matt couldn't miss her if he drove up. At five minutes to eleven, she went inside and ordered two coffees.

"I just heard about your new job," Millie said, snapping lids in place on the Styrofoam cups. "Sure surprised me. I figured you'd be going back to Hollywood with Luke John."

"Hollywood doesn't have a thing that interests me."

Millie eyed her curiously. "It's got Luke John Kendall."

"I know." Kelly smiled blandly, although her stomach felt a little queasy now. The wall clock said one minute until eleven. Where was he?

He would come! She repeated the assurance to herself over and over and then, to demonstrate her faith, told Millie she'd better go wait in the car for Matt. "We have a date to go parking."

Well, you've done it now, she scolded herself as she got back into the BMW. *You've jinxed it by telling someone.* Furthermore, if he stood her up, everyone in Weatherford would find out by noon tomorrow.

At four minutes after eleven, Kelly's head was starting to ache, and six minutes later she felt a heavy lump slide from her throat down to her chest. He wasn't going to come, and she might as well accept it. The longer she sat there, the more of a fool she would feel.

Blinking back tears, she started the car, switched on her lights and hurriedly backed out of the parking lot. Millie peered out the front window to watch her drive away, but Kelly didn't notice.

By the time she got home, her head throbbed and her throat was raw from crying. She took a couple of Tylenol, kicked off her shoes and went straight to bed, but she knew better than to think she could sleep. There was no use kidding herself any longer. It was really over. Her love affair with Matt had taken thirty years to get off the ground, but then it had soared for one short week. Soared and then crashed. She pulled a pillow over her head, wishing she could somehow wake up in July, when perhaps the worst of the hurting would be past.

11

AT FIRST SHE THOUGHT the pounding on her front door was part of a fragmented dream, but then Kelly realized she hadn't had time to go to sleep. She rolled over and sat up, listening to the racket. Maybe it was Jenny. Flipping on the lamp and squinting at the clock, she saw that only five minutes remained of the year. It would be just like Jenny to insist that Kelly not be alone at midnight tonight. Well, for once she'd just have to understand that Kelly *wanted* to be alone.

Spurred on by the noise, Kelly hurried through the house, turning on lights as she went, until she reached the entry hall. "Okay, Jenny, I hear you!" she protested as she swung open the door.

When she saw who stood on her porch, she said, "You!" and tried to slam the door in his face.

Matt was too quick for her. He pushed the door back open with one shoulder, stepping inside and closing it behind him before she knew what was happening.

"Damn you, get out of here," she muttered, reaching past him to open the door again.

He caught her by the arm and pulled her away, then leaned one hip against the door so there could be no question of her opening it.

Kelly stood there glaring at him, knowing she looked about as bad as she felt. She'd been huddled in bed fully dressed, crying her heart out for half an hour—long enough to wrinkle her white silk dress beyond redemption. Her hair was one wild tangle, her eyes were red, and her nose felt as if it was about to drip.

Matt, on the other hand, looked like God's gift to women. He wore tennis shoes, Levi's and a bright orange University of Texas sweatshirt, but he couldn't have been more handsome in black tie and tails. From his spun-silver hair to his Adidas, he was one sexy hunk, and it made Kelly ache just to look at him.

"I said get out of here," she repeated, hating the way her voice quivered. She ran the side of her hand across her damp cheeks and sniffled as quietly as she could.

"I believe we have a date tonight."

Her mouth fell open. The nerve of some people! "I believe you're mistaken."

"You're dressed for a date," he pointed out, sounding reasonable.

"*You're* not."

From his embarrassed glance at his clothes, she could tell he hadn't meant to keep their date. A knife twisted deep in her heart. "Would you please do us both a favor and go back home, or wherever you came from? I don't want to see you."

"Why not?"

Because it's killing me! "Because...because I'm sick."

Uh-oh! She knew the instant the words were out that she shouldn't have said that!

Matt straightened and stepped toward her, pressing his palm to her forehead. "What's the matter?"

"Nothing!" She jerked out of his reach. "Just a bug or something."

A trace of a smile tugged at the corners of his mouth. "It's a good thing I came. Obviously I'll have to stay all night and take care of you."

"Don't bet on it," she snapped, her frustration building. "Matt, I've asked you three times and I'm going to ask you once more. Will you get out of my house and out of my life?"

"No, I won't." His calm refusal amazed her. "Kelly, we did have a date tonight, and whether you like it or not I'm here to claim you."

He paused, glanced at his wristwatch and abruptly took her in his arms. His mouth descended on hers and blotted out her indignant objection with a kiss that began slowly and gained momentum until it had all the force of a tornado, sucking her into a maelstrom of heavenly sensations. As his mouth moved lazily on hers, his hands drew her closer, bestowing enticing caresses through the silk. His fingers spread on her tush and molded her to his hips with a subtle pressure that completely obliterated her willpower. Moaning, she melted against him, her hands winding around his neck even as his free hand massaged every bit of tension from her own neck and shoulders. Desire, hot and sweet, pulsed through her veins and made her weak.

When the kiss finally ended, she leaned limp and breathless against him, her mind struggling to recall what she'd been so mad about before he had launched his sneak attack.

"Happy New Year, Kelly," he murmured, his eyes smoldering as he smiled down into her dreamy face.

"Happy New Year, Matthew."

"About our date . . ."

Kelly stiffened and brought her arms down between them to push at his chest. "Oh, yes, our date."

He refused to let her go. "We do have a date, you know."

She lifted her chin, green eyes flashing. "We *had* a date. I was there. You didn't show up."

Tilting his head to one side, he studied her rebellious expression. Finally he asked, "Exactly how long did you wait for me?"

"You were supposed to be there at eleven. You hadn't come when I left at ten after."

His eyebrows rose. "You only waited ten minutes?" Assuming a wounded look, he added, "Have you ever known me to be on time for anything?" While she was still trying to remember if she had, he clicked his tongue in disappointment. "Kelly, I'm a doctor. No matter how hard I try to prevent it, my work interferes with my private life. I thought you knew that by now."

"You were working?" All her righteous anger fizzled. "Oh, Matt, I'm sorry." Her arms went back around him, and her tears returned. Hugging him, she buried her face in his shirt.

"Hey, come on, honey, don't do this," he said softly, pulling her close. "What's wrong?"

She wiped her eyes on his sleeve and sniffled. "It's just that I've missed you so much. I was so scared you wouldn't come tonight, and then you didn't—"

"Oh, babe, you don't know what scared is." He looked at her with undisguised anguish. "For all I knew, you were in L.A. at some hotshot party with Luke John tonight."

Kelly moved out of his grasp. "Uh, Matt, I want to tell you something that may or may not matter to you. I'm telling you just in case it matters." She faced him squarely. "There's nothing between Luke and me except friendship. Nothing."

From the taut expression on his face, she could see that it did matter a lot. "I'd like to believe you," he said slowly, "but that's not how it looked to me."

"Luke . . . that is, Luke and I wanted you to think we were attracted to each other, so we created an illusion to convince you."

"It looked pretty damn real to me."

She winced. "That's because Luke and I are both pretty damn good actors."

He drew in his breath, then let it out slowly. "Why?"

"Why try to fool you? Luke hoped you'd get jealous. He knew how I felt about you, and he figured it might make you want me, if you thought *he* wanted me. Personally I didn't have much faith that it would work, but at that point I was willing to try anything."

He swore under his breath. "You thought I needed a shove to start wanting you?" Running one hand through his shining hair, he demanded, "Did you imagine I spent that weekend with you just for the hell of it? Kelly, I've never wanted anyone as much as I wanted you!"

She swallowed with difficulty. "Not even Meredith?"

Matt looked taken aback. He blinked, brushed the back of his hand across his jaw and sighed. "Not even Meredith." They were definitely going to have to talk about Meredith.

"Then what made you stop wanting me?" Her voice was a pained whisper.

"I didn't stop!" He glanced around the small hallway distractedly. "Look, can I come in? I mean, all the way in? We really need to discuss **so**me things. I think I'd better straighten out a couple of your misconceptions."

What misconceptions could he possibly mean? Her nerves coiling tight again, Kelly led the way to the living room. "If you'll build a fire, Matthew, I'll go make coffee."

While it brewed, she washed her face and brushed out her hair into a curtain of burnished copper silk, then changed into a green satin robe. By then the coffee was ready. She took two cups into the living room and handed one to Matt, settling down into the opposite corner of the sofa from him. As she sipped from her mug, she wondered if Matt had any idea what he was doing to her pulse rate. Just the hint of his clean, distinct fragrance that reached her nostrils was enough to make her want to melt and slide down to his end of the couch and pour herself all over him. The firelight cast bronze shadows on his dark skin, accentuating his cheekbones and sensitive mouth, adding an aura of mystery to his eyes. Breathless, she reverted to staring at the fire. He seemed totally oblivious of her response to him, and she thought how odd it was that he could be so unconcerned with his good looks. Luke *always* noticed his effect on women.

Just then Matt put his cup down on the low coffee table and turned toward Kelly. He stretched out his arm along the back of the sofa so his hand almost reached her shoulder. "Kelly, I want you to know that when you came back here—when I spent those two days with you while you were sick—something happened to me that I hadn't expected. You touched me . . . somehow we connected. . . ." He seemed to be groping for words, finally shrugging in frustration. "I don't know how to put it exactly, but the thing is, I started to *feel* again. You brought me back to life. I began to want you with the kind of hunger that eats a man up from the inside, and

I never stopped wanting you for a minute. I want you so much right now that I hurt inside just thinking about it."

His husky words sent a thrill up her spine. "Oh, Matt, I want you too, more than you can ever know."

She started inching toward him, but he gestured her back with his hand. "Wait a minute. Let me finish. I don't just want you, I need you." Shaking his head, he frowned. "What I'm trying to say is, I *love* you." When his meaning registered, Kelly almost threw herself at him, but something in his eyes stopped her. "I don't love easily, Kelly—not this kind of love anyway. I tried not to feel this way, but I can't fight it anymore. If you want me, I'm yours."

Silently she reached out and placed her hand over his much larger one, a thousand love words trapped in her head, precariously balanced on the very tip of her tongue. He had more to say, and she needed to keep quiet and listen.

"I just ask one thing," he said hoarsely. "Before you answer me, be sure, be very sure that you know what you really want. Please don't keep me wondering if it's Luke John you're making love to when you're in my arms. I couldn't stand it again."

"You think...I use you as a...a substitute for Luke?"

"I'm not accusing you of anything. I'm only asking you to...to examine your feelings and see if this is a problem." Despite his soft tone, his hand clenched beneath hers. "Believe me, I wouldn't be doing you any favors if I played along with that kind of fantasy. Go ahead and accept the job at the college. Stay here and make a new career for yourself, if that's what you really want. I have no doubt you'll be a great drama instructor. Just make sure you realize from the start that I'm not Luke John Kendall."

Kelly stood up, reached for his hands and tugged him to his feet. Eyes wary, he watched her bring his right hand up to her mouth and kiss it, then repeat the gesture with his left. A bolt of hot desire lanced through him when her soft lips skimmed his knuckles.

"Three weeks ago I fell in love with a man," she said huskily, placing his hands on either side of her waist, keeping hers on top to hold him there. "He's so kind and beautiful on the inside that I'd love him even if he had an extra eye in the middle of his forehead." Her voice took on a sad note. "But the poor man has the misfortune to resemble a movie star, which naturally makes him wonder what part of him I really love."

Reaching up, she framed his face with both hands and touched her thumbs to the corners of the definitely sheepish, adorably crooked grin that was forming. "The truth, my gorgeous insecure darling, is that I love every inch, every pound, every last cell of you, inside and out." She spread one hand on the back of his head, her fingers tangling in his soft hair and urging him closer. When he bent his head, she gently blew aside the tousled curls on his temple and kissed the scar. "I love this body because you've lived in it for thirty-two years." Releasing his head, she slid her arms around his waist and pressed her mouth to his chest. The staccato pounding that she felt through layers of supple muscle and thick cotton made her lips tingle. "I love this heart because it's the very essence of Matthew Mark Kendall." She nuzzled him with her cheek. "*This* is how you're different. This heart prompted you to climb that windmill to return a sparrow's eggs after your brother robbed the nest." She lifted her head and met his quizzical gaze. "Grandma Bowen told me the whole story, but even before she did I was on to you. I could never mistake you for *anyone*." Her long dramatic pause gave emphasis to her next words. "There's only one surefire way to prove how much I adore you, though."

His eyes had started to sparkle. "Is that right? How?"

"By making mad, passionate love to you every single day for the rest of your life. Beginning now."

Her hands reached out to relieve him of his sweatshirt and collided with his fingers, which were moving to untie the sash of her robe. Somehow they managed to undress each other with minimal confusion and maximum arousal. Soon they lay on a downy soft quilt in front of the fire, light and shadows dancing across their golden nakedness as they merged.

He looped her hair back behind one ear to expose her neck and nibbled there so enticingly that chills skittered down her backbone. Kelly shivered and wound her arms behind his back, closing her eyes at the pleasurable sensations his warm skin produced everywhere he touched her. His hips glided in a provocative rhythm back and forth over hers, one strong-muscled thigh sandwiched between her long, slim legs. At the same time, his hair-dusted chest rubbed against her nipples, teasing a shocking response from the small, stiff buds. After a moment, he feathered his velvet lips down her throat to feast more aggressively on the firm, full mounds.

Gasping her approval, she arched backward to give him easier access to her tender breasts. To oblige her, he took one dusky crest into his mouth and suckled gently, causing wildfire to race out of control down the length of her body and scorch everything in its path.

"Matt...oh, Matt...I like this!" She ran her hands up and down his sides, exhilarated by the solid substance of his flesh and bone and muscle beneath her palms.

"So do I, honey." His tongue licked a moist, meandering path down to her belly and then back up to her collarbone. "I'm just not sure once a day for the rest of my life will be enough."

"We can always...negotiate." Slipping her hands past his waist, she clutched his taut buttocks and stopped his seductive hip-jiggling. The elusive torment it inspired was making her a little crazy. Demanding hands trapped him against her so she could savor the powerful evidence that his need was just as fierce as hers. She spread her legs to let him in, then hooked her feet around his hips to keep him there.

With one arm, Matt held her close, smoothing caresses over her damp, glowing skin with his other hand. He dropped small kisses on her forehead, her eyelids and her parted lips as he eased into the warm silken core of her femininity.

The desire that gripped him didn't quite block out his awareness of Kelly's slender frame beneath him. "Tell me if I hurt you," he said.

"The only way you could hurt me right now would be to stop, Matthew!"

He had no intention of stopping. He couldn't have stopped if he had wanted. Now that their bodies were joined, he resumed his electrifying thrusts, building tension between them until each was totally sensitized to the other. Every movement, every scent, every sound that touched them threatened to catapult them into orbit.

The fire finally did it. A log snapped in two, scattering hissing sparks and breaking Matt's concentration. He dropped down onto Kelly in momentary alarm, and she clung to him. His added weight upset the fragile balance of their passion, and they both teetered and fell over the edge of a cliff.

Stunned, they spiraled down through space together, their bodies intertwined and throbbing. Minutes passed before they hit bottom in a spectacularly satisfying, well-padded landing.

Kelly wiggled comfortably, her arms locked behind Matt's back. "Mmmm...now aren't you glad you watched the news tonight?"

"I didn't watch the news." Lately every time he turned on the TV, he saw Kelly with Luke John. It had gotten so painful that he'd decided he could live without the news.

"That's right, I forgot. You were at the hospital. So how'd you hear that I'm going to be working at the college?"

He wove his fingers in and out of her coppery tresses, totally absorbed in the silky feel of her hair. "I wasn't at the hospital tonight. I took your advice about occasional time off and worked out an agreement with some of my colleagues. I just happened to end up with forty-eight hours off."

"But...you said you were working!"

"I didn't actually *say* that, Kelly." He grinned wickedly, not in the least ashamed of himself. "I sort of let you think I had been working, so you wouldn't throw me out of the house."

She wondered whether or not to get mad. "If you weren't working, why weren't you on time for our date?"

"I, uh, didn't actually plan to keep our date, because I didn't think you would. Jenny and Mom both called to be sure I knew you hadn't gone back to L.A. and to tell me about your new job, but I figured you still wouldn't want to see me."

"Well, you showed up here, so something must have changed your mind."

"Your fan Millie did. She called and demanded to know why I was sitting around at home when the most terrific girl in the world was waiting for me at the Dairy Bar. Two minutes later, before I could even find my shoes, she called back and chewed me out royally because you had just driven off in shame, humiliated at being stood up." He chuckled. "Needless to say, I high-tailed it over here to try and get back in your good graces."

"Hmph! You seem to have succeeded rather deviously, I must say."

He gave her a look that could have melted butter. "Do you forgive me?"

"I shouldn't but . . . what the heck? I was always a sucker for your brown eyes, Matthew Kendall." She squeezed him hard. "I can't believe it took me thirty years to discover . . . mmm . . . *this*. Why did I have to spend my youth chasing someone who just looked like you?"

At her reference to Luke John, his muscles tightened instinctively and his stomach clenched into a familiar knot.

Feeling his response, she sighed. "You do that a lot, you know."

"Yes." He swallowed, thinking that he couldn't put this off any longer. "I have a . . . I guess you might call it a small problem with my brother."

"I've noticed."

He didn't seem to hear her wry comment. "When I found out for sure he was coming home for Christmas, I gave serious consideration to abducting you and hiding out somewhere in South America until the danger was past."

"What danger?"

"That you'd fall in love with him all over again." Before she could tell him how absurd that was, he released her and rolled onto his back. "But that's not my style. I just sat back and waited to get dumped. Again. No, that's not true. I didn't exactly wait, did I? I dumped you instead. I thought it wouldn't hurt as much that way." He gave a short, bitter laugh. "Boy, was I wrong! It hurt every bit as bad. This has been the worst two weeks of my life."

Kelly sat up and leaned over him, supporting herself on one arm, gazing down into his troubled eyes. "What do you mean, dumped again? Who dumped you?"

He looked straight up into her face, and she saw how difficult it was for him to answer. "Meredith."

"*Meredith*?"

He grimaced. "It surprised me, too, when she left, although I guess I should have been expecting it."

"But...why?" Kelly whispered, trying to absorb the astonishing news.

"Because making a marriage work takes time and effort from both partners. I don't know about Meredith, but I didn't have much energy left over after I put in twenty hours a day in classes and at the hospital. We shouldn't have gotten married in the first place. She was too young and I . . . I was just too wrapped up in medical school."

"You had to be in order to graduate." She laid a hand along his jaw. "I know you, Matt. You'd insist on learning everything they had to teach you so you could be the best doctor possible." Tracing his lower lip with her thumb, she thought about the pain he must have suffered all those years in silence. "How could she leave you? How could she stand to lose you?"

"I don't think she considered it much of a loss. She fell in love with someone else. Someone who could give her what she wanted." He paused. "At least she *thought* he could. By that time she'd realized she definitely didn't want to be a doctor's wife. And who could blame her?" His eyes darkened as he stared up at Kelly. "Do you know, she was gone twenty-four hours before I even missed her? I thought she was on a modeling assignment, or off visiting her friends or her parents or something. We didn't see much of each other because of my schedule." A self-mocking smile twisted his mouth. "Heaven knows how long I might have gone obliviously about my business if I hadn't come upon the note she left me. While I was still reeling from that shock, a policeman came to the apartment to tell me she'd been killed in a car accident in Tennessee."

Tears filled Kelly's eyes. "Matt, I'm sorry! How awful for you. It must have been hard to hold it inside all these years."

"I couldn't tell anyone. It would have torn everyone apart."

She grabbed his hand. "I agree that it probably would have been pointless to tell Meredith's parents what happened, but you should have at least told your own family. It might have helped a little to share it. They love you so much, Matt!"

"It would have killed them to find out the truth, Kelly." His voice was quiet. "They love Luke, too." Abruptly he pulled his hand free and sat up to face the fire, turning his back to Kelly. He bent one leg and propped his chin on his knee. "How could I tell them my wife had fallen in love with my brother?"

She felt as if someone had punched her in the stomach. "The other man was *Luke*?" Her heart aching for him, she scooted over behind Matt and slid her hands around his waist to give him a tight hug, her cheek pressed to his shoulder blade. "It doesn't make any sense, Matt. He may consider himself the world's greatest lover, but Luke wouldn't do that to you."

Matt sighed deeply, then turned to take Kelly into his arms and bury his face against her neck. "I know." His words were muffled. "He didn't know anything about Meredith's infatuation with him. He flirted with her the way he flirts with any beautiful woman, and she made the mistake of taking him seriously. She believed him when he said he'd get her a part in his next movie."

"Luke used that old line?" Kelly groaned. "Talk about corny!"

"I guess he made her feel special. He was just being nice to her because she was my wife, but she fell hard. Everything that she had once thought she felt for me, she transferred to Luke, and why not? He looked just like me, and he was charming to boot. He had an exciting life-style, money, fame. And he was fun. I spent all my time studying and working. One day she got tired of it and decided to take Luke up on his offer."

Kelly kissed the top of his silver-blond head tenderly. "Only she was killed before she got there, and you've kept quiet about it for seven years so Luke wouldn't feel responsible."

"Luke *wasn't* responsible. He had no idea she would misconstrue his flattery. He certainly didn't want her to leave me. If he did, he'd have told her he was going on location in Hawaii for six months. Meredith was killed driving to New York, where she assumed he still lived."

"So . . . do you feel responsible?"

"At one time I did, but somewhere down the line I realized that Meredith was ultimately responsible for her own life. I'm sorry the whole mess occurred, but my primary mistake was to marry her when I couldn't give her the attention she wanted. If I had held out for a year, our marriage probably never would have taken place, because she'd have lost interest in me and gone on to someone else."

Evidently Matt understood his spoiled bride perfectly, at least with the benefit of hindsight.

Kelly stirred in his arms and asked hesitantly, "If you don't blame Luke for what happened to Meredith, why are you so mad at him?"

He lifted his head and gazed into the fire. "I'm not mad at him."

"He thinks you are. You *act* like you are."

Shaking his head, he said, "I told you . . . I have this problem. For a year after it happened I was so torn up by the circumstances of her death that I couldn't talk to Luke at all because I was afraid I'd let something slip if I did. Even when I recovered from the shock I couldn't seem to get a handle on my relationship with Luke. I felt so damned inadequate. All my life people have compared the two of us, and I honestly never minded until my wife chose him over me."

"Your wife was incredibly foolish, Matthew. Her set of values stopped developing at puberty. Now my values, on the other hand, have matured nicely." She gave him a ferocious hug. "Don't you agree?"

"Oh, definitely." For the first time in an hour he felt like laughing. "Your set of values is one of the things I admire most about you."

He pulled her back down onto the quilt to show her some of the other things that he admired about her. The languorous demonstration proved so sensually enthralling that they lost track of time, and Matt finally had to pry himself away from Kelly and her admirable traits in order to throw another log on the dying fire.

When the flames had begun to leap and snap again, he knelt over her. "You're so beautiful," he whispered, having long since forgotten that he had once viewed her more objectively as "interesting."

She smiled to herself, partly out of amusement at his compliment, but mostly out of the sheer happiness that welled up inside her. "What are you doing?" she asked, getting up on one elbow to watch as he reached for his Levi's and fished around in one of the pockets.

He grunted, then broke into a grin when he pulled his hand out and closed his fingers around something small. He crawled back over to Kelly and picked up her left hand. "I was just looking for your Christmas present."

"Now, Matt... You didn't have to go out and buy me something just because my feelings got a little injured over that perfume." She flushed guiltily. "It was really a very nice gift."

One of his fair eyebrows shot up in amused skepticism. "Have you tried it?"

"Er, not yet." She wasn't about to tell him she'd poured the perfume down the bathroom drain the night he had given it to her.

Giving a knowing chuckle, he said, "I'm sorry I hurt your feelings. I asked Angela to run out and get you a present when I realized I couldn't give you what I'd bought for you the day we went shopping in Dallas...*this*." He waved his clenched hand in front of her. "No fancy wrapping this time, but—" he flattened his palm and revealed an exquisite diamond engagement ring "—if you'll agree to marry me, we can put this on your finger right now."

"Oh...oh...Matthew!" Tears sprang to her emerald eyes, and her voice trembled. She watched him slip the ring into place. "Oh, Matthew, yes! Yes, I'll marry you!" Crying in earnest now, she began beating his shoulder with her fists. "Why did you torment me? How could you have bought this and then not given it to me?"

He caught her in a tight embrace and kissed her wet cheeks, and together they fell back onto the rug. "I figured you'd rather have a ring from Luke." He raised his head and looked down at her with contrite brown eyes. "I was wrong...about a lot of things."

"Do you know how much I love you?"

"I'm beginning to learn."

"Do you trust me?" He nodded. "And Luke...do you trust him?"

Again Matt nodded, more slowly this time but no less emphatically.

"Then what do you intend to do about him?" Seeing Matt's perplexed frown, she said gently, "He's confused and hurt, Matt. He has no idea why you hate him."

"I don't—"

"I know, but he thinks you do. He misses you a lot. You were his best friend."

Matt rolled away from Kelly and got to his feet, his face a study of conflicting emotions. He took the jeans she held out to him and pulled them on as she donned her robe. Sitting down on the sofa, he propped his chin on his hands and stared at his bare feet. "I miss him, too." His voice was full of regret. "But I'm afraid it's too late."

She moved over to the stereo and raised the lid, then flipped a switch that set a record in motion. "Listen to this," she said. When he heard the opening notes of Luke's latest hit, he started to rise. But she gave his shoulder a shove, and he dropped back down, looking cornered. "Just listen, please, Matt. For once, listen to the words."

Kelly had heard the song hundreds of times in the past three weeks, at least fifty times since Luke had confessed to her that his only purpose in recording the ballad was to make Matt see how he was wasting his life. Now she watched Matt sit there in the magical firelight and listen to a message he could no longer avoid. Broad shoulders hunched, long legs outthrust, he resembled a modern-day, golden-haired Apollo whose lowered lashes couldn't hide the tears shimmering in his eyes.

But even as Kelly watched, even as Luke's mellow baritone filled the small house and feathered chills up and down her spine, Matt's face changed. Comprehension dawned slowly, so that by the time the song ended he was standing and looking at Kelly intently.

"Do you think maybe I could call him?"

"I think maybe you could." She rummaged through the drawer beneath the telephone for her address book. "In fact, I just happen to have his number here somewhere."

"It's not too late?"

Deliberately misunderstanding his meaning, she squinted at the clock on the mantel. "It's three-thirty here, which makes it one-thirty in L.A. That's late, but not too late. This is New Year's Day, after all. Besides, I think he'd want to take this call, no matter when it came."

Still he hesitated until Kelly picked up the receiver and handed it to him. "Shall I dial?"

"I'll do it." His fingers fumbled, and he had to start over, but finally he held the phone to his ear and listened to the distant summons. After a dozen rings, he figured his brother must still be out celebrating. Just as he started to hang up, the ringing stopped and Luke's familiar voice drawled hello.

Knees suddenly rubbery, he sank down on the sofa. "Luke, it's me. Matt." He swallowed. "Happy New Year."

Smiling, Kelly wandered out to the kitchen to reheat the coffee. She had poured two cups, had opened a tin of Christmas goodies and was preparing to behead a red-frosted Santa cookie when Matt spoke her name from the doorway.

She spun to face him and found him grinning, his arms spread wide.

Kelly ran into his embrace and felt herself lifted high, then pulled close to his hard, half-naked length. His mouth covered hers in a kiss that progressed rapidly from exuberant to tenderly grateful to subtly bewitching.

"Ahhh . . ." Kelly broke off, quivering inside. Much more of this and they'd be right back on the living room rug before she had a chance to find out how things stood between Matthew and Luke John. "I take it he was glad to hear from you?"

Matt laughed. "Stunned is more like it. It was a little awkward trying to talk to each other again, but we'll get better at it. He accepted my apology with more grace than I expected."

"You didn't tell him, did you?"

"No." His expression grew sober. "I'll never tell him about Meredith, Kelly."

She thought his decision was the best one for them all. She was just glad Matt had chosen to share the truth with her.

Hugging him, she muttered into his warm bare chest. "I want a wedding, and I want it quick!"

"Plan it however you like," he said expansively. "I've already bought the ring and lined up my best man."

"You mean Luke? He's coming back for it?"

"He says he wouldn't miss it."

"Terrific!" Kelly's imagination took flight. Slipping out of Matt's grasp, she motioned him over to the table and put the cookies and coffee in front of him, then sat down beside him. "Luke can double as soloist and serenade us with 'Here Comes the Bride.' We'll have the ceremony at the Dairy Bar—"

Munching on a Christmas tree, Matt eyed Kelly with apprehension. Was she kidding?

"—and of course it'll be televised. Jenny will be my matron of honor."

"Kelly! You want our wedding to be on television?" He sounded scandalized. "At the *Dairy Bar*?"

"Sure. Why not? If we invite Bo Hanover, he'll probably bring his camera whether we tell him to or not. And, let's see, we'll serve champagne and hot fudge sundaes at the reception." She smiled at him innocently. "Have I forgotten any details?"

Ah ha! he thought. *I'm on to you!* Kelly might have chosen a quiet life, but she could still manage to make things exciting for everyone—particularly him.

"If you have forgotten anything, I'm sure you'll remember in time to make this the event of the year in Weatherford," he said with dry humor. "Could you just grant me one small favor? Let's ask Millie to be the flower girl or something. I owe her."

"We both owe her. Okay, sure. Millie can sprinkle rose petals along our path or bear the rings or whatever makes you happy, my adorable husband-to-be."

His smile lit up his face. "Am I really adorable?"

Kelly's overwhelming love for Matt left her feeling as if her veins were flowing with molten honey. "You're not only adorable, you're irresistible."

"Oh, yeah?" A devilish gleam stole into his warm brown eyes. He stood up and pulled her to her feet. "Let's go and see about that."

"See about what?" she asked as he scooped her up and carried her back to their cozy pallet in front of the fire.

He knelt to put her down on the quilt and untied her satin robe, undressing her with a speed that only hinted at his growing passion. "Let's just see how irresistible I am."

Hastily ridding himself of his jeans, he lay down beside her and began touching her with skilled hands in places that were physically incapable of withstanding such potent magic. Her heart rate tripled, and her senses responded hungrily to his caresses. She felt gloriously alive, yet she could hardly catch her breath.

"Try, angel-witch," he teased her, his lips tickling her ear, his spun-silver, silky blond hair brushing her cheek, shooting darts of ecstasy through her heart. "Try as hard as you can to resist me, my beautiful love."

Kelly whispered a husky promise that she would try. She lied.

Harlequin Temptation

COMING NEXT MONTH

Take 4 books & a surprise gift FREE

SPECIAL LIMITED-TIME OFFER

Mail to **Harlequin Reader Service®**

In the U.S.
901 Fuhrmann Blvd.
P.O. Box 1394
Buffalo, N.Y. 14240-1394

In Canada
P.O. Box 609
Fort Erie, Ontario
L2A 9Z9

YES! Please send me 4 free Harlequin Presents® novels and my free surprise gift. Then send me 8 brand-new novels every month as they come off the presses. Bill me at the low price of $1.75 each ($1.95 in Canada)—a 11% saving off the retail price. There are no shipping, handling or other hidden costs. There is no minimum number of books I must purchase. I can always return a shipment and cancel at any time. Even if I never buy another book from Harlequin, the 4 free novels and the surprise gift are mine to keep forever.

Name _____ (PLEASE PRINT)

Address _____ Apt. No. _____

City _____ State/Prov. _____ Zip/Postal Code _____

This offer is limited to one order per household and not valid to present subscribers. Price is subject to change.   DOP-SUB-1RR

Harlequin Signature Edition

Violet Winspear

THE HONEYMOON

Blackmailed into marriage, a reluctant bride discovers intoxicating passion and heartbreaking doubt.

Is it Jorja or her resemblance to her sister that stirs Renzo Talmonte's desire?

A turbulent love story unfolds in the glorious tradition of Violet Winspear, *la grande dame* of romance fiction.

---

1. How do you rate _____
   (Please print book TITLE)

   1.6 ☐ excellent   .4 ☐ good   .2 ☐ not so good
   .5 ☐ very good   .3 ☐ fair   .1 ☐ poor

   EABC

2. How likely are you to purchase another book:
   in this *series* ?   by this *author* ?
   2.1 ☐ definitely would purchase   3.1 ☐ definitely would purchase
   .2 ☐ probably would puchase   .2 ☐ probably would puchase
   .3 ☐ probably would not purchase   .3 ☐ probably would not purchase
   .4 ☐ definitely would not purchase   .4 ☐ definitely would not purchase

3. How does this book compare with similar books you usually read?
   4.1 ☐ far better than others   .2 ☐ better than others   .3 ☐ about the
   .4 ☐ not as good   .5 ☐ definitely not as good   same

4. Please check the statements you feel best describe this book.
   5. ☐ Easy to read   6. ☐ Too much violence/anger
   7. ☐ Realistic conflict   8. ☐ Wholesome/not too sexy
   9. ☐ Too sexy   10. ☐ Interesting characters
   11. ☐ Original plot   12. ☐ Especially romantic
   13. ☐ Not enough humor   14. ☐ Difficult to read
   15. ☐ Didn't like the subject   16. ☐ Good humor in story
   17. ☐ Too predictable   18. ☐ Not enough description of setting
   19. ☐ Believable characters   20. ☐ Fast paced
   21. ☐ Couldn't put the book down   22. ☐ Heroine too juvenile/weak/silly
   23. ☐ Made me feel good   24. ☐ Too many foreign/unfamiliar words
   25. ☐ Hero too dominating   26. ☐ Too wholesome/not sexy enough
   27. ☐ Not enough romance   28. ☐ Liked the setting
   29. ☐ Ideal hero   30. ☐ Heroine too independent
   31. ☐ Slow moving   32. ☐ Unrealistic conflict
   33. ☐ Not enough suspense   34. ☐ Sensuous/not too sexy
   35. ☐ Liked the subject   36. ☐ Too much description of setting

5. What *most* prompted you to buy this book?
   37. ☐ Read others in series   38. ☐ Title   39. ☐ Cover art
   40. ☐ Friend's recommendation 41. ☐ Author   42. ☐ In-store display
   43. ☐ TV, radio or magazine ad 44. ☐ Price   45. ☐ Story outline
   46. ☐ Ad inside other books   47. ☐ Other _____ (please specify)

6. Please indicate how many romance paperbacks you read in a month.
   48.1 ☐ 1 to 4   .2 ☐ 5 to 10   .3 ☐ 11 to 15   .4 ☐ more than 15

7. Please indicate your sex and age group.
   49.1 ☐ Male   50.1 ☐ under 15   .3 ☐ 25-34   .5 ☐ 50-64
   .2 ☐ Female   .2 ☐ 15-24   .4 ☐ 35-49   .6 ☐ 65 or older

8. Have you any additional comments about this book?
   _____ (51)
   _____ (53)

Thank you for completing and returning this questionnaire.

PRINTED IN U.S.A.

NAME _____ (Please Print)

ADDRESS _____

CITY _____

ZIP CODE _____

BUSINESS REPLY MAIL

FIRST CLASS   PERMIT NO. 717   BUFFALO, NY

POSTAGE WILL BE PAID BY ADDRESSEE

NATIONAL READER SURVEYS

901 Fuhrmann Blvd.
P.O. Box 1395
Buffalo, N.Y. 14240-9961